WANDERING DOGIES

W. C. Tuttle

CENTER POINT LARGE PRINT
THORNDIKE, MAINE

This Center Point Large Print edition is published
in the year 2016 by arrangement with
Golden West Literary Agency.

First US edition: Houghton Mifflin.
First UK edition: Collins.

The text of this Large Print edition is unabridged.
In other aspects, this book may vary
from the original edition.
Printed in the United States of America
on permanent paper.
Set in 16-point Times New Roman type.

ISBN: 978-1-68324-182-9 (hardcover)
ISBN: 978-1-68324-186-7 (paperback)

Library of Congress Cataloging-in-Publication Data

Names: Tuttle, W. C. (Wilbur C.), 1883–1969, author.
Title: Wandering dogies / W. C. Tuttle.
Description: Center Point Large Print edition. | Thorndike, Maine :
Center Point Large Print, 2016.
Identifiers: LCCN 2016037646| ISBN 9781683241829 (hardcover :
alk. paper) | ISBN 9781683241867 (pbk. : alk. paper)
Subjects: LCSH: Large type books. | GSAFD: Western stories.
Classification: LCC PS3539.U988 W36 2016 | DDC 813/.52—dc23
LC record available at https://lccn.loc.gov/2016037646

M

WANDERING DOGIES

Center Point
Large Print

Also by W. C. Tuttle and available from Center Point Large Print:

The Redhead from Sun Dog

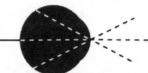

This Large Print Book carries the Seal of Approval of N.A.V.H.

I

Discharged

Gazing gloomily at the stack of letters on his desk, Orville Woodruff sighed dismally and shifted his eyes to the window, where he could look out at dingy housetops that stretched interminably, gray and uninteresting. For two years he had been cooped up in this office, taking verbal abuse from Henry Ellis, who was never satisfied.

Orville was only twenty-five. He was tall and awkward, with a thatch of red hair, a few freckles, wide blue eyes, and an extra-wide mouth that insisted on grinning in spite of Henry Ellis. Orville was secretary, bookkeeper, stenographer, and anything else that Henry Ellis might have for him to do to increase the business of Henry Ellis & Co., wholesale jewelers.

Orville was a dreamer of wide spaces, where he would not have to make pothooks and trial balances, before sweeping the office. Ellis's partner, Joe Buerman, who was the 'and company' of the firm, was somewhere on the Rogue River, angling for steelheads, and his colored post cards only accentuated the prisonlike atmosphere of the office. Orville liked Joe Buerman as much as he disliked Henry Ellis.

Orville was still staring out at the housetops when Henry Ellis came bustling in. Henry always bustled into the office. He came over and looked past Orville. Not seeing anything of interest, he sat down at his desk and looked indignantly at Orville.

'So!' he snorted. 'I am five minutes late, and I find you staring through a window. Nothing done. Mail not even sorted. Humpf!'

Orville sighed and picked up the stack of letters. 'Spring fever, I suppose, Mr. Ellis,' he said.

'Spring fever? I should pay you twenty-five dollars a week for having spring fever. Not even compensation insurance covers—'

'I'm sorry,' interrupted Orville, as he handed several personal letters to his employer. Henry Ellis always insisted on opening his personal letters. Henry Ellis grunted and then reached for a paper-cutter.

Orville was staring at a letter which had been forwarded to him from his former address. It was not for him, but for his mother—and she had been dead for over three years. The letter looked as though it had been badly handled. A glance at the postmark showed that it had been mailed in Encinitas, Arizona.

Encinitas! Something in that name struck a

chord in Orville's memory. Slowly he opened the letter. It was only a single page written in ink. It said:

DEAR MARY:

I've struck a bonanza at last, and the pot of gold at the end of the rainbow is in sight. Very soon I can repay you for the years of neglect—if riches can ever pay for that. You and Orville have suffered, I know, but that will soon be over. We will travel, see the world, and live like royalty. I will write you again in a few days.

Lovingly,

JACK

Orville lifted his amazed eyes and stared at the window. But he was not looking at the housetops. Suddenly, he was jerked back to earth by Henry Ellis's querulous, angry voice saying:

'Now you done it! You done it!'

'Huh?' queried Orville blankly. Henry Ellis was pointing a long, bony finger at him, his hand shaking in wrath.

'You—you dumb fool!' bellowed Henry Ellis. 'Not a brain in your head!'

Orville blinked. It seemed that Henry Ellis was angry about something.

'Yes, sir,' said Orville meekly.

'You unlimited fool! Do you know what you

done? Last week you wrote for me two letters. One you wrote to Joe Buerman, and the other you wrote to John Doyle, owner of Doyle's Jewelry Co., in Los Angeles—our best customer. Do you remember, you blunderer?'

'Why, yes, I remember.'

'So-o-o-o? Do you remember what I told Joe about Doyle?'

'Yes, I remember that you told him that John Doyle was a crooked Irishman, and that—'

'That's enough! You fool, you sent Joe's letter to Doyle! Here! He writes me, threatening suit for defamation of character. He says he never will buy from Henry Ellis again! Do you know what I am going to do to you?'

'Yes,' replied Orville, 'you are going to accept my resignation.'

Henry Ellis brushed a shaking hand across his face and sat down. Orville got up, covered his typewriter, and picked up his hat.

'What are you going to do?' asked Henry Ellis.

'The first thing I am going to do is to walk out of here, Mr. Ellis. The next thing I am going to do is to pay my room rent. Then I am going to buy a ticket to Encinitas, Arizona, and join my father, who has just struck it rich in a mine.'

'Rich in a mine? That is good. I am glad. If you don't have to work, maybe you won't make mistakes—but I doubt it. I don't owe you any-thing—I hope.'

'You paid me Saturday night, Mr. Ellis. This is Monday.'

'Blue Monday! Good-bye.'

Orville walked out of the office and took the elevator to the ground floor, where he halted to read the letter again. Where had his father been all these years?—he wondered. He tried to remember how many years it had been since his mother had heard from his father, Jack Woodruff, who had followed the lure of gold.

Slowly, Orville replaced the letter in the envelope. The address was a trifle dim, as though it had been written with weak ink. His eyes shifted to the postmark. Suddenly he sucked in a deep breath, shut his eyes for a moment, and then looked again. The postmark on that letter was fifteen years old!

'Fifteen years ago!' he gasped blankly.

'What was—your birthday?' queried a voice at his elbow, and he looked up to see Joe Buerman, bronzed, bewhiskered, fresh from the Oregon mountains.

Orville stared at him, as though at a perfect stranger. Buerman's smile faded, as he looked closely at Orville.

'What is wrong?' he asked gently. 'Somebody died?'

'I don't know,' muttered Orville. 'Oh—oh, hello, Mr. Buerman.'

'I should think you would,' laughed Buerman,

glancing at a clock in the lobby, and noting that it was not lunch time. 'Did Henry send you on an errand, or has something happened to Henry?'

'Something has happened to Henry,' replied Orville.

'Eh? Something happened? Tell me!'

'I have quit working for Henry.'

'You quit working for Henry? Well—is that all that has happened to Henry?'

'I—I think so. Was the fishing good?'

'Grand! The fishing was gorgeous. I wish I was back there. But why did you quit working for us, Orville?'

'I—I sent letters to the wrong persons.'

'You—oh, I see. Who got the other letter?'

'John Doyle, in Los Angeles. Henry—well, he told you what he thought of Doyle—and the letters got in the wrong envelopes.'

Joe Buerman choked with laughter. 'Doyle will get over it. Right to his face I have called him things that Henry couldn't even think to write. Come on back—I'll smooth Henry.'

Orville shook his head. 'Thank you very much, Mr. Buerman, but I am leaving town. I—I think I have a mine.'

'You think you have a mine? What sort of a mine?'

'I don't know. Have you ever heard of the pot of gold at the end of the rainbow?'

'The young feller,' declared Buerman soberly, 'is getting balmy.'

'I am really serious, Mr. Buerman.'

'You bet you are. You need treatments.'

'I—I expect to travel over the world and live like royalty.'

'Now listen, Orville,' pleaded Buerman, taking a gentle grip on his right sleeve. 'I'll betcha you're Napoleon—or something. You've got something—er—intangible, like rainbow gold, or something. That is great. I like you for it. But first you must see a doctor. I'll—'

'Why in the devil don't you come to work when you get back?' demanded Henry Ellis, who came from the elevator. 'I'm swamped, Joe. This brainless young man—'

'Hello, Henry!' exclaimed Buerman, releasing Orville, who went quickly out of the building and disappeared in the passing crowd.

Orville caught a street-car on the next corner and rode out to where he lived in a modest rooming-house. He did not have any idea what he was going to do. Because the boarders had the habit of looking over each other's mail, Orville had all letters sent to the office.

The fat landlady met him in the hallway. 'Home early, Mr. Woodruff.'

'I have been called away, Mrs. Millican,' he said. 'I am going to pack and leave at once.'

'Well, well! Bad news—or trouble?'

11

'Well, I—no, not trouble. I have heard from my father.'

'My Gawd!' Mrs. Millican stared at Orville. 'You—you told me that your father was dead years ago.'

'I believed that he was. He—he may be. That letter'—Orville drew a deep breath—'That letter was mailed fifteen years ago!'

'Why—where in the divil did it come from in fifteen years?'

'Somewhere in Arizona,' replied Orville.

'In Arizona? Sure, he must have mailed it in the shell of a turtle. Fifteen years? Well'—Mrs. Millican considered him seriously—'Well, did you answer it—yet?'

'I am going to answer it in person, Mrs. Millican.'

'Hm-m-m-m-m.' Mrs. Millican pursed her thin lips, crossed her arms over her expansive bosom, and squinted at Orville.

'I've had many a experience with mail goin' astray or not bein' delivered on the dot. And I've heard other folks swear that our postal department was too dumb to be in business—but you've got anythin' beat I ever heard. Fifteen years, eh? Fifteen years from Arizona to California. The next time I hear a postman whistle he may have a forty-year-old letter from my old man, who died in the wreck of the *Shamrock Lass* in the Baltic Sea. Anyway, it is worth lookin' forward to—

'cause I never knew what he did with his emerald-set cuff links.'

'I am sorry, Mrs. Millican,' said Orville.

'For bringin' up old memories?'

'No—for losing the cuff links.'

Orville went to his room and sat down on the bed, where he studied the letter all over again. He dug up some old maps and found Encinitas. It seemed like a tiny dot in a vast expanse of wide-open country. The country seemed sparsely populated, towns far apart, judging from the scale-of-miles on the map. He sighed and looked around at his few belongings.

'I hope,' he told the four walls, 'that no one down there needs a stenographer nor a book-keeper.'

II

Wandering Dogies

Spook Sullivan snored, snorted, and looked at the ceiling. Taking a deep breath, he turned over, yanked the blankets over his head, and made grunting noises. It was not daylight yet. From out in the kitchen came the rattling of pans, and 'Micky' Davis's clear tenor voice, singing:

'Give me my ranch and my cattle
Far from the big city's rattle.
Give me a big herd to battle,
For I just love herding cattle.'

It was the old Mexican song 'Rancho Grande,' sung in English. Spook grunted, snorted, cursed wearily, and sat up in bed. Spook was nearly seven feet tall and built on the specifications of a sand-hill crane. His face was long, his nose hooked, eyes small and sleepy; his mouth was wide and his neck extra long. His hair was long, and a lock of it hung over his left eye.

Swearing under his breath, he crawled slowly out of bed, yawned prodigiously, and proceeded to put on his shirt, overalls, and high-heeled boots. Then he yawned again, rolled a cigarette, and sat down on the edge of the bed. Finally he heaved a mighty sigh, got to his feet, and went into the kitchen, where Micky was frying bacon.

Micky Davis was of medium height, well-muscled, handsome; a happy-go-lucky type of Arizona cowboy. He had brown, curly hair, blue eyes, clean-cut features, and good teeth. His mother had been pure Irish, his father half Scotch.

'Put all the silver and cut glass on the table, Spook,' said Micky.

Spook yawned, tossed several tin plates on the table, and added some well-worn steel cutlery. A couple of tin cups completed the ensemble.

'I'm shore tired this mornin',' drawled Spook. 'Them damn Mexican calves acted like they didn't like *Estado Unidos*. I dunno—' Spook leaned against the newspapered wall of the kitchen. 'I never knowed anybody to make any money out of Mexican calves. You borrowed four thousand dollars from the Encinitas bank and paid the whole works for a couple hundred dogies.'

'Yeah,' said Micky, drawing back from the spluttering pan of bacon. 'Next fall I'll sell 'em for forty, fifty a head.'

'Mebbe,' drawled Spook. 'I still don't like it. You beat the Palos Verde Cattle Company in court, and gits title to this rancho. Fine. You know danged well that Flint Harper never forgets. I'll betcha Flint Harper owns stock in that Encinitas bank.'

'Well, suppose he does?' queried Micky, turning to the table.

'Uh-huh. Suppose he does! If anythin' happens to your investment they'll land on you with both feet. You'd be lucky to git out of here with your gun and bed roll. More'n one way to skin a cat, Micky.'

'Well, I'm not goin' to lose,' replied Micky. 'I'll keep what belongs to me, Spook. I've got that Palos Verde outfit licked.'

'I hope you're right—but I dunno.'

'Oh, quit lookin' for boogers,' said Micky, laughing. 'Set down and eat your breakfast, feller. We're brandin' calves all day—and it'll be hot.'

'That's right. I hate brandin' calves. Fact is, I hate work, but crave excitement; and there ain't no excitement in brandin' calves.'

'We won't worry about excitement,' said Micky, attacking his breakfast. 'I know danged well that I'll feel a lot better when the Bar D is decoratin' every one of them calves.'

'Two hundred,' sighed Spook. 'That's a lot of hide to burn. I wish I'd learned to be a doctor or a lawyer or somethin'. I wonder if it's hard to learn. I'd have been pretty good in school if it wasn't for arithmetic, gee-ography, and spellin'. I got sixty-five in readin' my last term.'

'Sixty-five ain't so much,' said Micky.

16

'Well, it's a hell of a lot when you figure I didn't score in anythin' else.'

'You'd make a fine doctor,' said Micky, grinning. 'One look at a dead man, and you'd die runnin'.'

'Yeah, that's right,' agreed Spook, who did not get his nickname for cold nerve.

They finished their breakfast, stacked the dishes on the table, grabbed their hats, and headed for the stable. Other business was more important than the housekeeping. The two hundred Mexican calves had been thrown into a fenced sixty acres near the ranch house, where there was a small branding corral.

Micky went to the corral, flung the gate open, and proceeded to build a small branding fire, while Spook rode away to pick up a bunch of calves. The sun was just peeping over the Smoke Tree range in the east. Spook seemed to be taking plenty of time in bringing in a few calves. Micky uncoiled his rope and hung it on the fence. Most of these calves were a little too big to flank, so there would be plenty of rope work.

But Spook did not bring any calves. He raced up beside the corral, drew up in a flurry of dust, and yelled at Micky:

'Fence cut at the far end; and there ain't a damn calf left!'

Micky picked up his rope and ran to his horse.

'Didn't you see *any?*' he asked.

'Not a dad-burned dogie! I'll betcha they drifted straight to that hole in the fence, and they've been gone all night. C'mon!'

'We're goin' back to the house,' said Micky, and Spook followed him at a swift gallop.

At the house they hesitated long enough to add rifles to their equipment, before heading into the hills beyond where the fence had been cut.

'Somebody used wire-cutters, then doubled the wire back so the calves wouldn't cut themselves,' explained Spook.

A mile beyond the cut fence Micky drew up and scanned the country. 'Plenty smart hombres,' he gritted. 'They fanned 'em out—so they don't show any trail. That was a gang job, Spook.'

'Shore looks like one. Where'll we go now?'

'One place is as good as another. Might go over in them breaks along Lobo Solo Canyon. If that damn bunch from the Circle H are mixed up in this deal, they might drift some of 'em that way.'

Micky was grim-faced, seething with anger. Four thousand dollars' worth of calves, scattered and at the mercy of anybody's running-iron.

'If Flint Harper is behind this move to break me, I'll drill his sour old hide,' declared Micky.

'Just like I told you—I'll bet he owns some of that bank at Encinitas,' said Spook. 'They was too damn anxious to loan you four thousand dollars. Hell, that's a lot of money.'

'More than I'll ever see again,' said Micky wearily.

Down in an old dry wash they found five tired yearlings. They worked them into a deep cut, where they managed to hold them and run on the Bar D brand. Dusty and drenched with perspiration, they rode on toward Lobo Solo Canyon. Riding out on a brushy mesa edge, Micky jerked his horse back and whirled the animal around.

'Two branders, workin' down in the cut!' he hissed to Spook, who dismounted quickly.

They jerked their rifles from the scabbards, and Micky led the way along the mesa to a washout, where they slid down, doubling low, as they advanced to the brush. The two men were at their right now. The smell of wood smoke was in the air.

'We've got 'em cold this time,' whispered Spook.

Micky nodded, his lips a grim line.

'If they make a break—shoot,' he said quietly.

They crawled to the edge of the brush. One man was crouching close to the calf, which was hog-tied. The roping horse was thirty feet away, keeping the rope tight. The other man was squatted at the branding fire, his hat on the back of his head. Against the edge of the brush stood another saddled horse. Somewhere a cow bawled softly.

'Don't move!' snapped Micky's voice. 'Keep your hands in sight, you damn slick-ears!'

The man at the fire jerked so quickly that his hat fell into the fire. The other man surged forward, both knees on the calf, as he turned his head. They were 'Frenchy' Allard and Bill Long, cowboys on the Box JB outfit. Frenchy Allard, at the fire, got quickly to his feet, ignoring his smoldering hat. The calf bawled painfully.

Before anyone could speak the brush crackled, and a big roan cow broke into the open, heading straight for Frenchy. With a yelp of fright he started to run, clawing for his gun, but it was no use, the cow was too fast.

Her head caught Frenchy about midway between his hips and his knees, from behind, lifted him off the ground, and flung him head over heels into the brush. Then it whirled and made for Bill Long, who made a dive for his horse. Bill stubbed his toe and went sprawling. The angry cow hooked viciously at him, but missed, because she had encountered the taut rope, and in making that twisting slash at Bill she had looped the rope around one horn.

The cow was rearing and bawling, trying to get loose, the horse was swinging around, keeping the rope tight on the old cow, and the calf was being dragged, bawling from fright.

'Shoot her, you damn fools!' howled Bill Long.

In spite of the fact that Micky and Spook came

down there to capture or kill a couple of rustlers, they were doubled up in the brush, fairly weeping with mirth. Then the rope broke, and the cow raced away, head and tail up, snorting and bawling. Frenchy stuck his head above the brush, and the air was blue with profanity. Bill Long sat up and pawed the dust out of his eyes.

'Jest what in hell was you fellers aimin' to do?' demanded Frenchy. 'My gosh, can't a feller brand his own calves without somebody hornin' in like that? I dang near got killed.'

'Look out!' yelled Spook. 'She's comin' back!'

Frenchy ducked back in the brush. Bill was on his feet, running toward his horse, as the old roan cow came galloping back. Micky and Spook went racing back to their horses, mounted quickly, and galloped across the mesa, where they halted and looked at each other.

'Mamma mine!' choked Spook. 'Wasn't that funny!'

' 'Course it was funny,' agreed Micky, tears running down his face. 'Bub-but it was their own calf! That cow wore the Box JB brand.'

'That's right,' gulped Spook. 'You know, when we was sneakin' down there I was goin' to say—'

'Wait a minute,' interrupted Micky. 'You never thought of sayin' anythin'.'

'Uh-huh. Well, anyway, I ain't so danged sure they knew who we was. The old cow shore took up a lot of their time. Man, I'd rather fight twin bulls than one mad cow. They're killers, Micky.'

'Yeah,' agreed Micky, looking back. 'I'll betcha Long and Allard are fit to be tied. Gosh, didn't that old cow lift Frenchy! That was fun.'

'You ain't forgettin' that we're still shy one hundred and ninety-five yearlin's, are you?' asked Spook.

'No; I can still remember that much, Spook. It looks like they took some of that herd over this way, because of us findin' them five. Anyway, we'll look over the breaks around Lobo Solo. Pickin' up one or two, here and there, might set us on the right trail.'

III

A Discovery

It was very brushy around the breaks near the big canyon, and the half-wild cattle hid in the heavy mesquite, while riders stayed to the wide trails. Old mossy-horned steers stayed in there, so tough of hide that mesquite thorns meant nothing to them.

Spook sent a small bunch of cattle out from a thicket, crashing toward the rim of the canyon. Micky, riding on higher ground, saw the cattle break around a deep washout. There was a spotted calf about six months old, that got bumped by a big steer, and was knocked head over heels into the washout. Micky rode quickly down near the washout, as Spook tore through the brush on the heels of the herd.

'No yearlin's in that bunch!' yelled Micky. Spook pulled up on the other side of the washout, and Micky told him about the calf.

'I can see him down there,' replied Spook.

The washout was about sixty feet in length, possibly thirty-five feet wide at the bottom, and about thirty feet deep on Spook's side. The sides were rather precipitous and brushy. On Micky's side the wall was limestone, broken and eroded, making it impossible for him to get down into the washout.

'Calf hurt any?' asked Micky.

'Guess not. Mebbe lost a hunk of hide. Ain't no brand on him either, but I seen the cow that's ma to him, and she's our critter.'

A few moments later Spook said, 'I've found a place where I can drag him out, I think. I'll tie off on my saddle horn and go down the rope. If it looks promisin' you can toss me your rope, and I'll tie 'em together.'

Micky took the rope off his saddle, dismounted, and squatted on his heels at the edge of the cliffs, while Spook worked his way down the rope to the bottom.

'I'll get him all right,' he called. 'Throw me your rope.'

Micky hurled the coil of rope, and Spook quickly ran out a small loop. The calf was unhurt, but frightened, judging from its bawling. As the calf raced past, Spook dabbed on the loop and turned the little fellow upside down.

'Ho-o-old fast!' roared Spook.

The calf bawled painfully.

The brush crashed at the upper end of the washout as the mother of the calf broke through the mesquite, looking for her offspring.

'You're all right,' called Micky. 'She can't come down.'

But Micky reckoned without the fighting

instinct of that old cow, which needed only an extra blat from the calf to cause her to dip over the edge and come down in a shower of sliding rocks, gravel, and dirt. She landed in a sitting position, fell over, got up, and headed for the luckless Spook, who had no place to go.

Micky saw him jump to a ledge of the sandstone just as a horn slashed against the soft rock, only inches away. There was a crevice, which Spook fell into, like a prairie dog going into its hole. The old cow whirled, looking wildly about for Spook, then trotted over to her calf, which was| on its feet, backing around in a circle.

Micky, doubled over again with mirth, saw a strange sight. With that mad cow in complete command of the washout, Spook Sullivan came out of the crevice, leaped far off the sandstone ledge, and went past that whirling cow so fast that the cow jumped aside. Spook headed for the place where he came down on the rope and went out of there with no assistance whatever except his churning feet.

Micky saw him go into the saddle and spur wildly away, without even picking up his rope. Micky's first thought was that Spook had been struck by a rattlesnake and was heading for help. There were plenty of rattlers in the breaks. Micky mounted quickly, crashed around the upper end of the washout, and traveled as swiftly as possible in the direction taken by Spook.

He found Spook less than a mile away. Spook tried to grin, but it was only a weak grimace.

'Had a hell of a time, didn't I?' he remarked nervously. 'What became of the cow?'

'You left her in the washout,' reminded Micky.

'Did I? Was she there when I came out?'

Micky looked curiously at Spook. 'What the hell happened to you?' he asked.

'Ma-a-an!' gasped Spook, and began rolling a cigarette with trembling fingers.

'Snake?' asked Micky.

'I—I hope to tell you—it wasn't no snake. Listen Micky; b-b-back there in that crevice—' Spook hesitated and drew a deep breath.

'Well, I—I got away from that cow. Then I kinda looked to see if I could get a little farther back, and I—I looked right square into the face of a skeleton.'

'Skeleton?'

'With a moldy old hat on. Grinnin' right in my face! Holy Mike! Wasn't over a foot away—grinnin'. Old, rotten clothes—jest a-hangin' on him.'

Spook shuddered and then scratched a match on his chaps.

'Mebbe it was your imagination,' suggested Micky.

'If it was,' replied Spook, 'I'd better git me a new one, 'cause my old one has shore gone cockeyed. No, I tell you, I seen him. He's kinda hunched forward in there, grinnin' under his hat.'

'We're goin' back and take a look,' declared Micky.

'*We!* Mebbe you're goin' to take a look, but I ain't. I'm jest as satisfied with one look as I would be with a hundred. I seen all there was to see, I'll tell you that much.'

'We've got to investigate,' said Micky.

'Investigate what? He's dead. Been dead a danged long time, if you ask me. Let him alone. I tell you, there ain't no luck in foolin' with skeletons. At least, I ain't never had no luck with 'em.'

'How many have you fooled with, Spook?'

'That ain't got a thing to do with it; it's the principle of the thing that don't appeal to me. Mebbe he caught a calf in that pothole and the old cow moved in on him.'

'Mebbe that's why he's grinnin' at you,' suggested Micky.

'Yea-a-ah! Well, you can laugh, if you want to. That danged old cow almost salivated me, I'll tell you that much. She shore put on her war paint before she slid down that bank. Not only that, but she's a Circle H calf. I was mistaken in the brand.'

'You can do as you please,' said Micky, 'but I'm goin' back and have a look at that skeleton.'

'Well, I'll go back, but I won't look.'

•••

Micky led the way back to the edge of the washout. The cow and calf were gone, the rope tangled on a snag down in the washout.

'Old range cow could git out of a well,' declared Spook.

Micky lost no time in sliding down into the washout, while Spook sat on the edge and offered sarcastic advice.

Even knowing exactly what to expect, Micky was a little startled as he gazed upon the remains. Sheltered from the elements, the clothing of the skeleton had molded and rotted. It was faded almost to the color of the sandstone. A section of stone tilted across the lap of the skeleton held it in a half-sitting position. Debris had piled up around the boots, covering them about halfway to the tops.

The bone-handled butt of a revolver protruded from the rubble, and Micky dug it out. It was a Colt .45, rusted and filled with dirt. There was something else that seemed foreign to that spot. Pieces of rock—reddish quartz; pieces about as big as eggs. Possibly half a dozen chunks. Micky blew the dust off one piece.

'Gold!' he gasped. 'Rotten with yellow gold!'

He put the pieces in his pockets and began a closer examination. There was something scratched on the sandstone on a level with the skeleton's head. It was not scratched deeply. It read:

28

That was all. Likely the last word was meant to be 'murdered,' but had been left unfinished because the man was unable to scratch more. Micky flung the end of a rope to Spook, and scrambled back to the top.

'Do you still think I was lyin' to you?' asked Spook.

'He's there all right. Spook, did you ever hear of a man named Jack Woodruff?'

'Nope, I don't reckon I ever did, Micky. Didja find that gun down there? Man, that's shore plugged plenty. What's that?'

Micky drew out a piece of the ore and handed it to Spook.

'Take a look at it,' suggested Micky.

'Sufferin' Moses!' exclaimed Spook. 'It's gold!'

'The skeleton had it in his pockets, Spook. You can see where the weight of it broke through the rotten cloth.'

'I'll be a stepson to a sidewinder! But what about that name?'

'Well,' said Micky, 'that name was scratched on the sandstone. It looks to me as though this feller had been shot and hid in that crevice. Mebbe he knew he was dyin' when he wrote who he was on the stone, and he died before he could tell who killed him. He started to write the word "murdered," but didn't quite make the last letter.

I reckon that me and you better go over to Encinitas and notify the sheriff. We won't say anythin' about the gun and ore. Anyway, the gun is only a souvenir—and I'd shore like to know where that ore came from.'

'Mebbe that's why he was killed,' said Spook.

'You mean—somebody else wanted to know where he found it?'

'Uh-huh. Anyway, somebody around this country might remember who he was. How long do you reckon he's been dead, Micky?'

'Judgin' from surface indications, he's been dead a long time.'

'We want to see the sheriff, anyway,' remarked Spook. 'He ought to know about them missin' yearlin's.'

'That's right,' nodded Micky. 'I'd forgotten them already.'

Bill Long sat down on the ground beside the remains of the branding fire and cursed long and fervently. He invoked all the wrath of the Hereafter against—somebody. Bill had been battered all over, the latigo on his saddle had been busted in the struggle between cow and horse, and Frenchy was somewhere out in the brush trying to capture Bill's horse.

With skinned hands he patched up the latigo, perspiration running off his long nose, his eyes blinking out accumulated dust. The old cow was gone, taking most of Bill's new rope. Frenchy was mad, too. He had untied the calf, tried to boot it in the rear as a sort of parting salute, missed his kick, and gone on the back of his neck in the hot coals of the branding fire.

Bill looked up balefully as Frenchy came back, leading the horse, which had a horn mark along its left side where the angry cow had slashed in parting. Frenchy drew up, caressing his scorched neck. Frenchy had a long, turkeylike neck, which had been generously scorched.

'I'm so damn mad that I could bite a cow right in two,' declared Frenchy. 'If I even had any idea who them two fools was, I'd shoot their damned livers loose.'

'Damn near killed me,' said Bill hoarsely. 'Hooked me, goin' and comin'. Didn't you'—Bill got creakingly to his feet—'see 'em?'

'Not clear,' groaned Frenchy. 'The first cowboy comedian I hear, I'll kill him, if I hang for it, Bill. My Gawd, that old critter was on the prod. Do yuh know, the back of my neck is burned clean of hair. I can still smell it burnin'.'

Bill groaned as he saddled his horse. Every joint in his body ached.

'They done acted like we was misbrandin' somethin', Frenchy.'

Frenchy tried to laugh, but his neck hurt.

'It startled me,' he admitted. 'F'r a moment I wasn't sure what I was doin'. Look at m' hat, will

31

yuh? It's a good thing I kicked it out of the fire when that old cow charged, or I'd be half out of hats right now.'

'I dunno,' said Bill, testing his cinch carefully. 'It could have been Buck Bramer and Skee Harris, or it could have been a couple o' them sidewinders from the Harper outfit. No tellin' who it was.'

'Or mebbe Micky Davis and Spook Sullivan,' added Frenchy.

'I never thought of them two. Yeah, mebbe it was.'

'Well, yuh can see how damned easy it would be for a feller to git himself caught if he was misbrandin' somethin', Bill.'

'That's right. Well, there's no use of us brandin' any more calves today; so we might as well go to town. I could shore use a lot of whisky right now.'

'A dash of liniment wouldn't hurt me,' declared Frenchy. 'That old cow shore boosted me into the brush. Don't say nothin', Bill. Somebody is bound to find it out from the fellers that done it to us—and then they better look out, eh?'

'If you think I'm goin' to forgit it—yo're crazy. Let's go.'

The sheriff, 'Buck' Bramer, was a huge man, wide of girth, with a full-moon face, small eyes, and a walrus mustache. 'Skee' Harris, the deputy was so nicknamed, because of having the longest feet in the country. He was less than six feet tall, scrawny, with a long neck, hatchet face, and a tired, drawling voice.

With the two officers in their office was Duncan Wheeler, owner of the Box JB outfit. In the boom mining days of Smoke Tree Valley, Wheeler had been an assayer. He still owned a little assay office, where he pottered with furnace and test tubes once in a while.

Duncan Wheeler was several inches over six feet in height, very thin, long-armed, long-legged. His long face was deeply lined, extremely sad most of the time, and his head was bald, except for a fringe around his big ears and down the back of his neck.

The three men were conversing in the sheriff's office at Encinitas when Micky and Spook tied their horses and came in.

'We ain't hornin' in on anythin' private, are we?' asked Micky.

'Come right in, Davis,' invited the sheriff genially. 'What's on your mind?'

'Plenty,' said Micky. 'Yesterday evenin' we threw two hundred head of yearlin's into my fenced sixty, intendin' to start markin' 'em this mornin'. Some dirty rustlers cut the fence and— they were all gone this mornin'.'

'No!' exclaimed the sheriff. 'Every one gone?'

'Cleaned out,' nodded Micky grimly. 'We range-branded five head over near Lobo Solo Canyon. That's all we found so far.'

'Well, by golly, that needs investigatin'!'

'Was them the Mexican yearlin's you bought?' asked Wheeler.

Micky nodded. 'Looks like somebody's tryin' to break me.'

'I don't know who—' began the sheriff.

'Yuh don't need to say that, Buck,' Micky interrupted quickly. 'How much stock does Flint Harper own in the Encinitas bank?'

'You're barkin' up the wrong tree, Micky.'

'It's the only tree in sight. I borrowed four thousand from that bank. If I can't cash in on them calves, I'm sunk.'

'Flint Harper's too big to do a thing like that,' drawled Skee Harris. 'He don't need your money.'

'That's your opinion, Skee.'

Micky turned and looked at Duncan Wheeler.

'Dunc, you've been in this country a long time. Did you ever hear of a man named Jack Woodruff?'

'Woodruff?' Wheeler placed a huge hand across his mouth, his fingers scratching at his stubbled chin, his eyes closed.

'Woodruff? It seems to me that I did. Lemme see-e-e—Woodruff? Why, there was a feller around here, years ago—yeah, I believe his name was Jack Woodruff.'

'How long ago?' asked Micky.

'How long ago? Why, it must have been twelve-fifteen years ago. I'd plumb forgot him.'

'Disappeared, didn't he?'

'Did he? Well, I dunno if he disappeared or not. Folks have a habit of comin' and goin', you know. What about him, Davis?'

'We found him today.'

'You found him?'

'I found him,' corrected Spook.

The sheriff and deputy were interested now.

Micky explained how Spook discovered the skeleton. He did not say anything about the gun nor the samples of gold ore.

'Well, we've got to get him out of there and give him a decent burial,' said Duncan Wheeler. 'Wasn't there anythin' to show how he died?'

'I reckon he was murdered, Dunc.'

'We'll determine that later,' said the sheriff. 'I suppose we better take the coroner along. Can you find the place again, Davis?'

'That won't be hard to do,' replied Micky.

They walked out of the office, where they met the old postmaster, bringing a letter which he handed to the sheriff.

'You ought to put stamps on it, Buck,' he smiled.

'That's some more of Skee's brilliant work,' said the sheriff.

'I reckon I forgot to stamp it,' admitted Skee. 'I mostly always do. Mr. Evans, you've been here a long time. Did you ever know a man named Jack Woodruff who was here ten, twelve years ago?'

The old postmaster scratched his chin thoughtfully.

'I've been thinkin' about that name,' he said. 'I don't just remember him clear. But a week or two ago we was buildin' a new counter in the post office, and behind the old one I found a letter that had fallen there against the wall. It was directed to someone named Woodruff. I dunno who sent it.'

'Must be a different Woodruff,' said the sheriff. This'n has been dead for years.'

'It wasn't sent to a man,' smiled the postmaster. 'Mary Woodruff, I believe was the name. Yeah, I kinda remember a feller of that name—but it was years ago.'

'A prospector or a miner?'

'I don't remember that much about him. There were lots of miners and prospectors around here fifteen years ago.'

'We better take several ropes along,' said Micky. 'He won't be easy to take out of there.'

While the sheriff and deputy were preparing to go after the skeleton, Frenchy Allard and Bill Long rode into town and tied their horses at the rack in front of the Smoke Tree Saloon. Getting off their horses seemed a painful operation, and they went into the saloon walking like two very, very old men, suffering from rheumatism.

Duncan Wheeler rode over to the saloon and

went inside. Micky and Spook looked at each other tearfully.

'I reckon the old cow caught 'em,' remarked Spook.

'They shore look all run down,' agreed Micky.

Duncan Wheeler came back and joined the cavalcade.

'I thought I'd get Frenchy and Bill to go with us,' he said, 'but they said they hadn't lost any skeleton.'

'They walked kinda crippled,' said Spook soberly.

'Yeah. Said a proddy old cow caught 'em brandin' a calf.'

'They can shore put on in the sere and yaller leaf awful quick,' said Spook. 'Still, it's kinda funny for a couple old hands lettin' a cow run a blazer on 'em.'

'Uh-huh,' agreed Wheeler dryly. 'I guess maybe their mind wasn't on their work.'

All of them, except Spook, went down into the washout. There was little difficulty in removing the skeleton from the crevice. They dug away all the rubble, but found nothing that might have fallen from the rotted pockets. In fact, the remains showed nothing that would absolutely identify the man who had died in the crevice. There were only the scratches on the sandstone. There were the leather cartridge belt, half-filled with badly corroded cartridges, an empty holster, shrunken and twisted from age and weather.

'I reckon we'll have to call him Jack Woodruff and bury what's left,' said the sheriff. 'Mebbe he was murdered all right. The left arm was broken. There might have been bullets in the body, too. If we'd screen out that sand and gravel, we might find 'em.'

'Not much use of doin' that,' said Duncan Wheeler. 'No use tryin' to prove anythin' at this late date. What happened must have happened fifteen years ago, at least. Prob'ly a fight between prospectors.'

Micky and Spook did not go to town with them, but searched for calves all the way back to the Bar D, and finding none. After supper, they examined the samples of gold ore, which were almost too rich to be real.

'It was funny about that postmaster findin' a letter addressed to a woman named Woodruff,' said Spook. 'Found it behind their old counter when they tore it away. Micky, do you suppose that letter has been there all them years?'

'I suppose it could.'

'Man, I'd like to have that letter. It might tell where this gold came from. I'd like to be rich—once. Wouldn't you like to be able to walk in that bank and tell 'em to take the danged ranch?'

'I might have to,' sighed Micky, 'whether I'm able or not.'

IV

The Winner!

Orville Woodruff took a morning train out of San Francisco. After the shock of discovering that the letter was fifteen years old had passed, he decided to go anyway. He had saved some money—enough to enable him to try and find some trace of his father—so he bought a ticket to Sierra Vista, which was the nearest railroad point to Encinitas.

Across the aisle from him was a very attractive girl. To Orville she looked very well dressed and extremely good-looking. Orville had always been too busy to bother about girls. In fact, he was just a trifle girl-shy. But this girl seemed so whole-some and friendly that Orville nodded to her and said, 'Good morning.'

The girl replied, 'Good morning.'

Then they both smiled.

When Orville smiled it was almost from ear to ear. He said, 'Isn't it funny?'

'What is funny?' asked the girl.

'Me saying good morning to you—and I never saw you before.'

'I don't know,' said the girl, smiling. 'I hate to ride hours and hours and never speak to anyone except the conductor or the porters.'

'I am going to Arizona,' said Orville. 'I believe the town is called Sierra Vista.'

The girl's eyes widened a trifle.

'Why, so am I!' she exclaimed. 'My home is at Encinitas.'

Orville moved into the seat opposite her. 'My name is Woodruff—Orville Woodruff.'

'Mine is Norma Harper, Mr. Woodruff.'

'Isn't that fine?' smiled Orville. Norma Harper. I—I wonder if you know my father—or knew him. His name is Jack Woodruff.'

'No, I don't believe I do. In fact, I do not believe I have ever known anyone by that name in Smoke Tree Valley.'

Orville sighed deeply and looked out the window. 'He was a miner, I believe.'

'There isn't any active mining going on in the valley now,' she said. 'The mines never were a great success.'

'I—I got a letter from him,' said Orville. 'He said he had struck a very rich mine.'

'Wouldn't that be wonderful!' exclaimed Norma. 'My father owns a lot of property in the valley, including the Circle H outfit, known as the Palos Verde Cattle Company.'

'You have been visiting in San Francisco?' he asked.

40

'I have been attending the university. This is my second year.'

'Second year? And there was I, living across the bay all that time!'

They both laughed.

Orville was curious about Smoke Tree Valley, so Norma told him about her life on the Circle H, how they handled cattle, broke horses, and did the hundred-and-one things required in running a cattle ranch.

She mentioned Micky Davis several times, and Orville wanted to know who Micky Davis might be.

'He used to work for my father,' she told Orville. 'Before that we went to school together. Micky and Dad had trouble. Well, it wasn't exactly trouble, either. Micky wanted to marry me, so Dad fired Micky and sent me to college.'

'Fortunately,' said Orville dryly.

'Not for Dad. You see, the Palos Verde Cattle Company owns and controls a lot of acreage in Smoke Tree Valley. Years ago somebody nested on a piece of land almost due south of our home ranch. They were forced off. Others moved in—but got out. Dad is a sudden sort of a person.

'After Dad fired Micky and sent me to college, Micky filed on this ranch as a homestead, and claimed part of the open range. Micky wasn't the kind you can run out of any place, so it was taken to court, and it was settled in favor of

Micky. He registered the Bar D brand, and became a full-fledged cattleman.'

'I suppose he wrote to you,' sighed Orville.

'For a long time, he did. Dad wrote and told me that Micky had a woman in Mexico. He was taking presents down to her. I wrote and asked him if he was taking presents to a woman in Mexico, and he said he was. Micky is very honest. After that I sent his letters back unopened.'

'That wasn't very kind of your father, Miss Harper.'

'Don't you think it was better—to know it at once?'

'Perhaps. But still, your father doesn't like Micky Davis.'

'I believe,' said Norma, 'that we won't discuss Micky Davis any longer. What is your business, Mr. Woodruff?'

'I am the most remarkable bookkeeper in the world, Miss Harper.'

'In what way?'

'I can add up a simple column of figures six times, get a different answer every time—and not one will be correct.'

'Have you that sort of a recommendation from your last employer?' asked Norma soberly.

'No,' replied Orville. 'I was afraid to wait until he wrote one.'

Norma looked sharply at him.

'Did he fire you?' she asked.

'I resigned ahead of it,' smiled Orville. 'Really, I am glad it happened. Miss Harper, you do not know of any firm in Arizona who might need a combination bookkeeper, stenographer and—and floor-sweeper, do you?'

'No, I do not, Mr. Woodruff.'

'Thank you. I also hope that no one else does. You see, I hate that sort of work. But one must eat, I suppose.'

'What sort of work are you seeking in Arizona?'

'I haven't any idea. Primarily, I am seeking my father. His letter says he has struck a rich mine—a pot of gold at the end of the rainbow. He wrote'—Orville drew a deep breath—'that he would make up for all neglect to Mother and me; that we would live like royalty—now.'

'You haven't seen him for a long time?' asked Norma.

'Many years. I do not know how many, Miss Harper. In fact I hardly remember him. He had the wanderlust, I suppose. It was hard on my mother. I am twenty-five now. Mother died over three years ago.'

'Do you mean that your father—after all these years—and doesn't he know that your mother is gone?'

'I don't know. For years she did not know where he was—long before she died—when I was a little shaver.'

'It must be a new strike at Encinitas,' said

Norma. 'No one mentioned it to me in letters. When did your father write you?'

'The letter was to Mother,' replied Orville. 'I received it yesterday—but it was written fifteen years ago.'

Norma looked at him, a puzzled expression in her eyes.

'Written fifteen years ago?'

'Postmarked at Encinitas fifteen years ago!'

'It sounds impossible.'

'It may be,' sighed Orville, 'but I am going to find out.'

They arrived in Sierra Vista next morning. Flint Harper was at the depot to meet Norma. Harper was a big, rawboned man, hard-faced, with eyes the color of cold steel. He kissed Norma and looked sharply at Orville, who carried her baggage.

'Dad, this is Orville Woodruff,' said Norma.

'Howdy,' said Flint Harper coldly. 'Woodruff?'

'Yes,' said Norma. 'His father owns a rich mine somewhere around this country, and Orville is looking for him.'

Flint Harper's eyes narrowed in thought for several moments. Then he took the baggage from Orville and turned away.

'Buckboard's over this way, Norma,' he said, walking away.

Norma smiled at Orville and said quietly, 'I

may see you in Encinitas,' before following her father to the buckboard.

Sierra Vista was a shipping center for cattle. It had all the appearances of having started out to be a little city but decided to remain a cow town. Orville had never seen so many saddled horses in his life as were lined along the hitch racks. He went to the nearest hotel, registered, then went out to see the town. The hotel clerk told him that there was a stage for Encinitas, which left Sierra Vista at seven o'clock, arriving at Encinitas about midnight.

Norma and her father drove from the depot down to the center of town, stopping at a general store for some things which her father had ordered. Duncan Wheeler, Bill Long, and Frenchy Allard were in front of the store, and Wheeler came over to shake hands with Norma.

'You're shore lookin' fine,' he told Norma. 'You get prettier every day. Your father will have to build a hog-tight fence to keep the cowboys away from the Circle H, once they see you.'

Duncan laughed and walked into the store with Flint Harper. Norma noticed that Long and Allard both limped as they went across the street to a saloon. Norma did not know either of them, as they had come to Smoke Tree Valley after she went away last year.

Orville rarely took a drink, but somewhere he had heard that it was an insult to a cowboy to refuse to drink with him. He strolled into a saloon. Several cowboys were at the bar. One big, hairy cowpuncher looked at Orville and gasped:

'Who the hell ordered fire?'

'Hyah, Red,' chuckled a small, bow-legged cowboy. 'Have a drink?'

'Why, yes, I believe I will,' replied Orville.

'Wheel out another scoop, bartender,' ordered Shorty. He turned to Orville and shook his head warningly. 'Drink her quick, and don't get it near your hair, pardner. The stuff they sell here is almost pure benzine.'

'There ain't nothin' better in Arizona,' declared the bartender.

'Fer settin' a fire,' added the short cowboy. 'How'd it taste, Red?'

Orville gulped, gasped, and wiped away the tears.

'How on earth do they keep it corked?' he gasped.

'That's been a question for years,' said the hairy one. 'It's my turn to ruin a few stummicks. Keep your money in your pocket, Red. Your turn comes next.'

After four drinks of that liquid dynamite, Orville grew expansive. He added a reedy tenor to a song, and was loudly congratulated by the rest of the boys.

'You and that feller McCormack sing a hell of a lot alike, Red.'

'My name is Orville,' corrected the inebriated newcomer.

'Sh-h-h!' warned Shorty. 'My gosh, don't let that git out!'

'It is my name,' insisted Orville. 'Orville Woodruff.'

'Nature,' said the hairy one, 'is sometimes unkind.'

'Nature didn't have nothin' to do with his name,' said Shorty.

'I wasn't thinkin' of his name. Imagine a feller with hair like that named Orville! Where at have you been all your life, Orville?'

'San Francisco,' replied Orville. 'I am a book-keeper.'

'Jest like Shorty,' said the hairy one. 'He kept mine.'

'Have you books to keep?' asked Orville wonderingly.

'I did have. It was called "The Confessions of a Countess." '

'Let's have another drink,' suggested Shorty. 'The trouble with you is that every time you get a few drinks under your belt you talk about that book. Hell, you can't even read. Don't pay any attention to him—uh—what did you say your name was?'

'Orville Woodruff. My father—' Orville hesitated, swallowed, and took a deep breath. He wanted to get this straight.

'Your father what?' asked Shorty.

'He—he dishcovered gold mine. Oh, ver', ver' rich. Tha's why I am here.'

'Where at's this here gold mine?' asked Shorty. Orville looked owlishly at his own reflection in the fly-specked bar mirror.

'That,' replied Orville thickly, 'is a shecret.'

Things became blurred for Orville. He had little recollection of anything that happened, except that somebody helped him onto the seven o'clock stage. Being the only passenger, Alex Bowden, the driver, looked him over, decided that he was too drunk to ride outside, and shut the door.

About halfway to Encinitas, at the bottom of a long climb over some stiff grades, the stage always stopped at Pancho's Place. It gave the team a breathing spell before the hard climb, and it also gave the passengers a chance to sample Pancho's whisky, coffee, or to have a bite to eat.

Alex Bowden tried to arouse the snoring Orville, but to no avail; so he left his passenger there and went into Pancho's Place. The stage usually stayed fifteen to thirty minutes.

But Orville was not destined to sleep during that intermission. With no ceremony whatever he was gagged, bound, blindfolded, then taken from the stage and carried away from there. He was placed on a saddle, tied, and speedily taken away. Alex Bowden came from Pancho's Place, got on his seat, and drove away, supposing, of course, that his passenger was still asleep in the stage.

It was decidedly a new sensation for Orville, who had never been on a horse, much less gagged and bound to a horse. The sensation of going up and down hill, together with his already upset stomach, wasn't a happy experience. Gradually he sobered to a realization of his predicament, but without any understanding why such things had happened to him.

He seemed to be going forever through brush. Finally he went down and down, until it seemed to Orville that the horse would never get on even keel again. At last he reached the bottom, and in about five minutes more was stopped. Someone untied Orville's legs, which were so stiff that he had to be helped from the saddle. He was led stumbling along for about fifty paces, then he was unceremoniously set down on solid rock, and the covering was taken off his eyes. He was relieved when they took the gag out of his mouth, but was unable to speak.

On one side of a small fire stood a blackened coffee-pot. They seemed to be in the mouth of a cave. Three masked men stared at Orville in the flickering light that threw huge shadows on the rocky walls.

'Well, that much is done,' remarked one of the men thankfully.

'We better pull out,' suggested the other.

49

'Yeah, I reckon so. Watch this feller, Mex. We may not be back before tomorrow night.'

'I watch heem,' said the third masked man, a short, stocky person.

'See that you do.'

The two men walked out, and Orville heard them ride away. The Mexican helped himself to a tin cupful of coffee, drank noisily, then kicked a chunk of mesquite root into the dying fire. Picking up a blanket, the Mexican wrapped it around himself and sat down across the fire from Orville. A rifle lay across the Mexican's lap.

'You mind your own damn beesness,' he told Orville.

The order was so ridiculous that Orville, even in his misery, had to laugh. The Mexican fondled the rifle suggestively.

'I'm theenk you are damn smart, eh?' he remarked.

'At present you must be the judge,' mumbled Orville painfully.

'Shut up! I'm mak' you tired leestening.'

'Perhaps if you tied my hands in front of me I might be able to lie down,' suggested Orville.

'You theenk I geeve damn w'at you do?'

'I think you are a fine fellow,' said Orville.

'I theenk you are damn liar.'

'I bow to superior knowledge. I wish you'd tell me why I was brought here.'

'I don't know.'

'Who were the two men who brought me here?'

'I don't know.'

'I see,' said Orville wearily. 'You just live here and take care of anybody they happen to bring along.'

'I no leeve here. Shut up! You are tired from leestening.'

Orville hunched his shoulders against the rock, and in moving his numbed arms he discovered that his right wrist was rather loose in the rope. Working carefully, without using enough action to attract the Mexican guard, he finally got his right hand loose.

What good this was going to do, Orville did not know. He hunched there, suffering the pains of returning circulation in an arm that seemed sound asleep. He was able to shift the left one to a different position, although it did not seem to be part of him at all.

The guard, hunched against the wall, stirred occasionally. Finally, he kicked more wood on the dwindling fire.

'I would like to have a drink of water,' said Orville.

'You theenk I'm go hell of a long ways for water—for you?'

'I could drink a little coffee.'

'*Madre de Dios*!' exclaimed the Mexican. 'You theenk you are boss from me? *Americano,* you make me seek.'

'I'm sorry,' said Orville.

'W'at the hell you sorree about, eh?'

'Oh, just sorry I make you sick. Wouldn't you give me just a sip of coffee?'

'Seep?'

'Just a little in a cup.'

The Mexican shrugged his shoulders, picked up the pot and shook it carefully before he poured a little in a battered cup. Then he tested the temperature with a grimy forefinger.

'*Poco caliente*,' he said, and came over to Orville. Clinging to his trailing blanket with one hand, he leaned over and held the cup toward Orville's lips.

As Orville leaned forward, he reached out with his right arm, wrapped it around the Mexican's legs behind his knees, and threw himself forward. With a yell of fright the Mexican went over backwards, flinging the cup against the rocky ceiling of the cave.

For several moments they were in a kicking, flailing heap. Orville, unused to combat, failed to take advantage of being on top. The Mexican kicked loose and made a mad scramble for the rifle. But Orville grasped the guard's left ankle and reared back. Orville's left hand was loose in the ropes, but he was having trouble in releasing it.

The Mexican was kicking backwards with his free foot, but doing no damage. Then Orville got his left hand loose and grasped the flailing foot. It was a sort óf stalemate. The Mexican was helpless, but Orville didn't know what to do next.

Finally he saw a way out of the situation. Getting slowly to his feet, Orville had the Mexican in the position of a wheelbarrow. Then he shoved forward, sprawling the Mexican on his face, and darted for the rifle, only to trip on the rope, which was still around his waist, and go sprawling himself.

They were about equal distance from the rifle now. Slowly they got to their knees, watching each other closely. Then the Mexican fairly leaped to his feet and dived at Orville, who moved quick enough to avoid the weight of the Mexican's dive. Again they were both on the floor, locked in combat.

There was no conversation, no sound, except the slither of their clothes on the stone floor, and their heavy breathing. The Mexican succeeded in getting a throat hold on Orville, but the redhead shoved a knee into the Mexican's midriff, breaking the hold. Then they both got to their feet. Orville was the taller, but the Mexican was heavier. Perhaps the Mexican held the advantage, because the redhead had never been in physical combat.

Suddenly the Mexican rushed in, head down, and Orville slugged him square in the nose with his right fist. It was the thrill of a lifetime to Orville, as he felt that fast smack into yielding flesh. The Mexican wavered and staggered aside, his mask torn away.

But the Mexican was not whipped. He came back, swinging with both fists, and one of them landed just above Orville's left eye, starting the blood. Orville went back a step or two, breathing heavily. The Mexican followed up his seeming advantage, only to get a solid right in the mouth before he cut Orville's lower lip with a glancing punch. That right to the mouth flung the Mexican aside, spitting teeth, and Orville dived into him. The force of the impact sent them both against the rocky wall. Orville was nearly knocked out when his cheek crashed into the rock; but the Mexican's head landed solidly, and he slumped to the floor—cold.

Orville staggered around, hardly able to breathe, and so tired he could barely brace his feet and keep upright. His mind flashed back to a prize fight he had seen—a knock-out finish. He lifted his own tired, right arm, and gasped wearily:

'The winnah! Red Woodruff!'

Then he leaned against the wall and laughed foolishly. The Mexican had not moved. Orville picked up the coffee-pot and drank the bitter mixture as though it was nectar of the gods. Blood was running down his temple and down his chin, but he did not mind.

Gingerly, he picked up the rifle and looked it over. He had never fired a rifle in his life; didn't even know how to operate one. So he took it by the stock and proceeded to hammer it over a projecting rock, until the barrels were a decided arc. Then he flung it aside.

Swaggering just a trifle, he walked out from under that roof and looked up at the stars. Behind him was a solid wall. Straight in front of him was another wall. Only overhead could he see the starlit sky. A horse nickered softly, and Orville jerked around. It was off to his right. He went back to the fire, picked up a flaming piece of root, and walked out there again.

It ceased to flame when he took it away from the fire, so he picked a tuft of coarse grass and lighted it. Under an overhanging slab of sandstone stood a saddled horse. There was no bridle, but a rope tied the animal to a projecting chunk of rock. It was rather a nondescript creature, and the saddle was old and patched.

Orville extinguished the fire, went cautiously in and untied the rope. The horse seemed gentle and friendly. After due deliberation, Orville decided to get into the saddle. It was comparatively easy, and he felt a friendly glow toward this member of the horse kingdom.

'There still remains a certain question,' said Orville aloud. 'Do you know how to get out of here, horse? If you do, I am ready.'

As though with complete understanding, the horse turned around and started away in the darkness.

V

A Lady Gets A Present

Micky Davis and Spook Sullivan spent a futile day searching for yearlings. They came home tired and discouraged. The day's work had netted them exactly three yearlings, which now gave them a grand total of eight out of a possible two hundred.

'Well, Micky, it's just like you said,' remarked Spook, as they ate a cold supper that night.

'Just like I said what?' queried Micky.

'You've got the Palos Verde Cattle Company whipped.'

'I reckon that's once I spoke out loud in church,' sighed Micky.

'Well, you've still got your youth and stren'th.'

'Do you know—I've been doin' a little thinkin' about this deal, Spook.'

'Well, I wouldn't let it ruin me mentally,' said Spook soberly.

'Listen to me, you cockeyed ghost dancer. What would be more simple than for Flint Harper to make a deal with Miguel Topete?'

'You mean—for Topete to drift that bunch back across the border?'

'And throw 'em right back on his own range again. Who could ever prove that I owned 'em? Miguel is as crooked as a snake. On a deal with Harper, he could turn right around and hand 'em over to Harper, and nobody would ever be the wiser.'

'And you'd be broke, Micky.'

'That seems to be the idea.'

'I wish,' said Spook wearily, 'that we knew where that skeleton found that gold mine.'

Micky nodded thoughtfully as he rolled a smoke.

'I reckon we'll go down into Mexico tomorrow,' he said. 'Mebbe *Abuela* Ramirez knows some-thin'.'

'Who'd tell Grandma Ramirez anythin'?'

'Well, that son of hers, Manuel, ain't no saint, Spook.'

'I hope to tell you he ain't. Well, let's slosh off the pans and roll up a little shut-eye; I'm tired.'

The next morning they were out early. Just out of curiosity, Micky decided to circle around past the washout where they had found the skeleton. Spook voted against it, but went along, grumbling at the waste of time. He held the horses, while Micky went down there.

Someone had been there, using a piece of screen to examine the rubble in the crevice, and had thrown the screen aside. Micky decided that the sheriff had done this, looking for bullets.

There was to be an inquest, but the sheriff had not notified Micky and Spook as to when this was to be held.

They went on to Encinitas, where Micky purchased several yards of the gayest calico in the store. Then they rode due south to the border, which was only marked by posts. Farther to the east was Mesquite, a little port of entry, but they had nothing to declare except their few yards of calico.

Two miles below the border they came to a small group of tumbledown shacks, where innumerable goats browsed. The buildings were little better than exaggerated packing-boxes patched with tin. Out in the yard sat an ancient Mexican woman in a crude chair. She was Grandma Ramirez, reputed to be well over a hundred years old.

'*Amigo mio*,' she chuckled, as Micky and Spook came across the low fence. '*Buenas dias.*'

'Hyah, *Abuela*,' laughed Micky. 'How's the world treatin' you?'

'*Poco buena.* I theenk I 'ave w'at Manuel say ees rheuma—rheuma—'

'Rheumatism?' queried Micky.

'*Si, si.*'

'You're too young to have rheumatism. Only old folks have that.'

'You've got growin' pains,' said Spook, squatting on his heels and rolling a cigarette.

Micky gave her the present, and she opened it with trembling fingers. Micky never forgot her. Her old eyes lighted with joy when she beheld all those bright colors. Her gnarled old hands caressed it lovingly.

'*Gracias*, Micky,' she said.

'Aw, that's all right. Where's Manuel?'

'*Quién sabe*? Two, t'ree day he no come home.'

'Have you seen Topete lately?'

She shook her head, as she examined the cloth.

'I bought two hundred calves from Topete.'

'Manuel tell me.'

'Somebody cut my corral fence and stole all of 'em, *Abuela.*'

She lifted her eyes and looked keenly at him.

'All gone?' she asked, and he nodded.

'*Mucho dinero*?' she questioned.

'Eight thousand pesos. *Oche millares.*'

'*Por Dios*! W'at you theenk, Meeky?'

'I think that Topete stole 'em back from me.'

After several moments of deep concentration she said:

'Manuel work for Topete.'

'I know it.'

'*Madre de Dios*!' she exclaimed softly. 'There ees no church, no padre, and I am too poor to buy candles. All I can do is pray over my poor beads.'

'I don't blame Manuel,' said Micky. 'He is paid

by Topete. There would be no blame on Manuel, if—well, if I was sure Topete stole my cattle.'

'Manuel ees my son. If he is sober, he tells notheeng. I shall pray he come home drunk, Meeky.'

'Well, that's fine, *Abuela*. We'll be goin'—and I'm glad you like the present. Young ladies like you shore can wear colors.'

'*Gracias, gracias*,' she said, smiling. '*Vaya con Dios*.'

'I allus like to hear her say that, Micky,' said Spook, as they rode back toward the border.

'What does it mean?'

'Go with God. It's better'n any of us Americanos say. We usually say, "Don't take any wooden nickels." '

'She's a great old lady, Spook. She hid me five days in her shack while all the damned rurales in the country were tryin' to find me—the time I had to gun down that crazy, marijuana-smokin' Mexican. I can't never do enough for her. She's human—that's all.'

'Not so awful ignorant either, Micky.'

'I hope to tell you she ain't ignorant. And I found out later that the Mexican was her nephew. She knew it at the time. I asked her later and she said she did, but that he was a marijuana smoker.'

'My gosh, what have we in view!' exclaimed Spook.

It was Orville Woodruff, coming up the trail on

that old horse he had borrowed in the canyon. Orville was really a sight. One eye was almost closed, his left cheek swollen, his upper lip swollen. He was hatless, almost shirtless, his thatch of red hair stood on end, like the comb of a fighting rooster.

Micky and Spook drew up, looking him over critically. Orville eyed them with a wide, twisted grin.

'Thank goodness, I've found somebody!' he exclaimed.

'So have we,' replied Spook.

'This equine,' stated Orville, pointing at the drooping ears of his steed, 'seems inclined to wander. We have spent over half of the night and all of the morning trying to find someone. Where are we?'

'Right now, you're in Mexico,' said Micky.

'Mexico? I must have gone farther than I thought. I really have no business in Mexico.'

Micky, suppressing a smile, proceeded to examine the horse.

'That looks a lot like Manuel Ramirez's horse, Spook,' he said.

'I was thinkin' the same thing. Where'd you get the horse, Red?'

Orville smiled. 'Isn't it queer—everyone calls me "Red." My name is Orville.'

'Red fits you a lot better,' said Micky. 'What's your last name?'

'My full name is Orville Woodruff.'

Micky and Spook looked closely at Orville, then looked at each other. Woodruff! The name scratched on the sandstone.

'You—you didn't ride down into Arizona on *that* horse,' said Spook.

'No, indeed, I did not. I—I acquired this horse last night.'

'Bought it?'

'No, I didn't buy it.'

Orville drew a deep breath and looked at the sore knuckles on his right hand.

'I fought for it,' he finished. 'That is—I won the fight and took the horse.'

'I'd like to know what the other feller looks like—if you won,' said Spook soberly. 'You're a sight.'

'I imagine that I do look rather worn,' said Orville, grinning.

'Well, just who was you lookin' for?' asked Micky.

'I—well, I started for Encinitas. Someone took me off the stage, tied me all up, and lashed me to a horse. I haven't any idea where they took me. However, there were three masked men. Two went away, leaving me and the third man. I presume he is a Mexican. However, I got one hand loose, and I assure you we had quite a fight. I believe I won, because he was unable to continue. So I took the only horse and came away.'

'My gosh!' gasped Spook. 'Didja ever see such hair on a dog?'

'There was no dog,' said Orville. 'At least, I never saw one.'

'You say your name is Woodruff?' queried Micky.

'Yes, sir, Orville Woodruff.'

'That's fine,' said Micky. 'My name's Micky Davis, and this person is known as Spook Sullivan.'

'Micky Davis? Why, you are the cowboy that Norma Harper—you see, she—'

'Who?' interrupted Micky.

'Norma Harper. She was on the train to Sierra Vista, where her father—'

'Norma Harper came to Sierra Vista and her father met her? When was that?'

'Really, I'm not sure, but I believe it was yesterday.'

'Uh-huh,' drawled Micky. 'You've known her quite a while?'

'Since day before yesterday. We were on the same train and—'

'Wait a minute,' interrupted Micky. 'Your face needs a little fixin', so we better head for the ranch. No use of you goin' to Encinitas in that condition, and we've got plenty room.'

'I hope you have water at your ranch,' said Orville. 'I—I really need a drink.'

'We'll cut past Juniper Spring,' said Spook. 'It's only a couple miles—and I'm dry, too.'

• • •

They took Orville to the ranch, washed his wounds, dressed them as well as they could, filled him with food and put him to bed. Then Micky and Spook went out on the porch, where they sprawled in the shade and considered the situation.

'Why didn't you find out more about the feller?' asked Spook.

'Wait'll he gets back on his feet. I've got a feelin' that he's some relation to this Jack Woodruff, but I can't quite figure out what he's doin' down here. And why on earth would somebody kidnap him off the stage?'

'Yeah,' drawled Spook, 'and I've got to set around on pins and needles waitin' for that jasper to wake up and talk about it. Micky, do you suppose he knows anythin' about that gold?'

'How could he?'

'Wait a minute, pardner. Remember that letter— the one to Mary Woodruff? Mebbe there is a Mary Woodruff. Mebbe this feller—Say! That letter might have told where the gold was found!'

'It might,' agreed Micky. 'I never thought of that.'

'I guess I'm not so dog-gone dumb.'

'Well, don't dislocate a shoulder tryin' to pat yourself on the back,' advised Micky. 'Even if he does know where the gold is, it isn't *our* gold.'

'You can shore think of the most discouragin'

things, Micky. If he should happen to—Here comes Skee Harris!'

The deputy sheriff rode up to the house, looked them over soberly, looped a leg around his saddle horn, and yawned wearily.

'Didja ever try sleepin' for that, Skee?' asked Spook.

'You don't happen to have any use for a skeleton, have you?' he asked.

'I hope to tell you I haven't,' said Spook quickly.

'You ain't tryin' to give one away, are you?' asked Micky.

'No, I ain't,' replied Skee. 'I'm tryin' to *find* it.'

'*Find* it?' gasped Spook.

'Yeah, it's gone.'

Micky sat up straight and stared at the deputy sheriff. 'Are you jokin', Skee?' he asked.

'Hope to die if I am. Doc sewed it all up in a canvas and put it in a locked shed back of his house, waitin' for the inquest. Well, it's gone. Not only that, but yesterday a young feller boarded the stage at Sierra Vista. He was pretty drunk, says Alex Bowden. At Pancho's Place, Alex asked him to get out, but the feller was asleep. When the stage got to Encinitas, this young man ain't on board. Me and Buck have been ridin' all the rest of the night tryin' to find him.'

'Well, can you tie that one!' exclaimed Spook. 'Who was the feller?'

'Alex didn't know. Said he came in on the train

and proceeded to get drunk. Some cowpunchers helped him on the stage, and Alex says they made him hold the stage until they sung a song.'

'I've allus said,' declared Spook, 'that you never can tell what's goin' to happen next in Arizony. When's the inquest, Skee?'

'When we find that skeleton.'

'Did Doc decide that the feller had been shot?' asked Micky.

'Doc didn't decide nothin'. How can you decide anythin' about a feller when his outside is off and his insides are out?'

'I guess that's right, too. Buck went out and sifted the dirt in that crevice where we found the skeleton, didn't he?'

'Huh? Sifted the dirt? What for?'

'Mebbe he was lookin' for bullets.'

'Hell, no! I don't reckon Buck ever thought of doin' that.'

'Oh! Well, I just wondered if he did.'

'Naw. Why, that feller's been dead for years. I don't see why we should have an inquest. You can look at the remains and know blame well he's dead.'

'You say you can *look* at the remains?' queried Spook.

'Well, you could, if we could find the remains, Spook.'

'Yeah, I guess you could. I know blame well I had my look.'

'There must be somebody playin' a joke on you,' said Micky. 'Nobody would want a skeleton. What could you do with one?'

'You might use it to scare Spook with,' said Skee, grinning.

'Yeah, and I ain't denyin' it,' said Spook quickly. 'Show me one of them things, and I'll run so damn fast that I hum like a spike.'

'Gettin' any trace of your missin' calves, Micky?' asked Skee.

'I've found eight out of two hundred.'

'Not such a good average. Well, I've got to be travelin', gents. I'll see you later.'

This being Saturday evening, Micky decided to ride to Encinitas and hear what was being done about the missing skeleton and the missing young man. Spook stayed home with Orville, who was still asleep.

Encinitas was thronged with people doing their trading, drinking and gambling. Micky listened to the gossip, and it seemed to be the general opinion that someone had stolen the skeleton as a joke on the sheriff. As to the missing young man, many believed that the stage driver had been drunk and imagined he had a passenger.

Several men stopped Micky and asked him about his calves, assuring him that they were on the lookout for them. One grizzled cowboy from the north end of the county complained drawlingly:

'When I heard about them two hundred yearlin's

gettin' away from you, Micky, I tied my runnin' iron on my saddle and headed down thisaway. I've been a-ridin' for two hull days, lookin' and a-lookin', but I ain't even had occasion to build me a brandin' fire.'

'I suppose you was going to run my Bar D on 'em wasn't you, Mose?' asked Micky.

'Well, I'll tell you,' drawled Mose. 'I ain't never had much eddication, and I don't know one letter from another. My own brand is a Wet Moon, kinda like a hunk of watermelon. I can draw her purty good.'

'I'll say you can,' drawled a voice at the bar, and in the general laugh Micky went outside. He crossed the street to a general store, and came face to face with Flint Harper. The big cattleman tried to brush past Micky, but the young man blocked him. The buzz of conversation in the place halted.

'I've been waitin' for a chance to tell you a few things, Flint,' said Micky, his voice as brittle as thin ice. 'When you couldn't beat me in court, you used your influence at the bank to get me a loan of four thousand dollars, knowin' that I wanted to buy Mexican calves. Then you framed up with that cheatin' Topete to cut my fence and steal all my calves, knowin' that it would break me, and you might be able to take back the Bar D through the bank. I just wanted to tell you that I know this, Flint, so we'll be even to start with.'

Flint Harper's face was white, his eyes blazing

with wrath. His big right hand, dangling near his holstered gun, was opening and closing spasmodically.

'Reach for it,' said Micky quietly. 'I'm accusin' you of bein' as crooked as a snake; so you've got a reason to reach for your gun.'

It was a tense situation. They were not over three feet apart; they couldn't miss. If Flint Harper's hand jerked toward his gun, it might mean death for both of them. They all knew that Micky was fast with a gun—as fast as Flint Harper.

'No!' whispered a voice. 'No, Dad!'

Micky's eyes shifted a fraction. Norma had stepped from behind some men, her face white, eyes wide, as she whispered her appeal to her father. Flint Harper relaxed slowly.

'I reckon we'll postpone this, Davis,' he said huskily.

'Suits me,' nodded Micky. 'Make your own dates.'

Flint Harper motioned Norma toward the doorway and followed her outside. She turned and looked back at Micky, but his back was still turned. After several moments, Micky walked slowly along the counter to where the proprietor stood.

'Give me a package of tobacco, Jim,' he said.

The man handed him the tobacco and said:

'Thunder, that was close, Micky!'

'Prob'ly be a hell of a lot closer before it's settled,' replied Micky calmly, and he walked out.

Norma and her father went straight to their buckboard. Flint Harper yanked the tie ropes off and fairly flung himself into the seat. They drove out of town in a shower of dust and gravel. Not until Flint Harper drew the team to a more sedate pace was there any conversation.

'Dad, is there any truth in what Micky said?' Norma asked.

'Do you think I'm a crook?' he countered savagely. 'That young fool needs a lesson.'

'A lesson in what?' asked Norma.

'Openly accusin' *me* of stealin' his cattle!' snapped Flint Harper. 'I won't have it! I'll run him out of Smoke Tree Valley. I'll show him.'

'Did Topete take his calves, Dad?'

'Did—How do I know? I'm not Topete's confessor. Great heavens, you're not upholdin' Davis, are you, Norma?'

'I'd like to know the truth, Dad.'

'I haven't got his calves.'

'He didn't say you had. He said you schemed with Topete to—'

'I never schemed with Topete. That's a lie.'

'Have you any interest in the Encinitas bank, Dad?'

' "My interest" in the bank ain't got a thing to do with it. If they wanted to give Davis four thousand

70

dollars on a mortgage, that was their business.'

'Did that mortgage also cover the two hundred calves, Dad?'

'No, it didn't; it was only on the Bar D ranch.'

'Did they show it to you before letting him have it?'

Flint Harper snorted softly. 'You ought to be studyin' law.'

Norma was silent until just before they reached home, when she said:

'Dad, have you ever seen the woman Micky went to see in Mexico?'

'No,' he said sharply. 'I don't even know who she is.'

'Are you sure he went to see one?'

'I only know what I've been told. There wouldn't be any reason to lie to me about it.'

'Are you immune, Dad?'

'Immune from what?'

'Having people lie to you.'

'What are they doin' to you in school—teachin' you how to argue?'

'Teaching us how to reason, perhaps.'

'Well, I wouldn't carry it too far,' advised her father.

When they were back at the ranch Norma went to her father in the big main room of the house, where he was sitting glowering at the floor.

'I'm sorry I argued with you, Dad,' she said. 'I know I should hate Micky Davis.'

'I don't ask you to hate him, Norma. I don't know if I hate him, or not. Damn it, he gets under my skin. He beat me in court, and he has an idea that he can keep on beatin' me. Imagine the young fool openly accusin' me of stealin' his calves. Why should I steal his calves?'

'To break him, I suppose,' said Norma.

'But I don't care if he never goes broke, Norma.'

'You wouldn't want him to build up a herd on the ranch he beat you out of in court, would you, Dad?'

Flint Harper looked keenly at his daughter.

'I still think you should study law,' he said. 'Yo're allus tryin' to trip me up. Darned if I don't believe you think I helped steal Micky Davis's calves. Just because I have bought Mexican calves from Topete—well, I *bought* 'em, that's all. I'm not askin' that fat-headed bandit to do my dirty work. All right, smarty, go ahead and ask me if I'd rather have an Americano do my dirty work.'

'I wasn't going to ask you that, Dad.'

'No? Well, I haven't any dirty work to be done.'

'I wish you could convince Micky Davis of that.'

'I don't care whether he's convinced or not. He don't mean a darn thing to me—except to irritate me. I'd sooner have a boil.'

'And to think that I almost married him, Dad.'

72

'There yuh go again! Let's forget Micky Davis.'

'All right,' smiled Norma. 'He has lost all his calves, the bank will foreclose on his ranch—and you can get it back—cheap. They do sell cheap to stockholders, don't they, Dad?'

'How do I know? I never bought anything from the bank.'

Norma changed the subject, much to Flint Harper's relief.

'Dad, what did you think of Orville Woodruff?'

'I haven't thought much about him, Norma. I wonder what became of him. Headin' for here, wasn't he?'

'Yes. He was looking for his father, I believe.'

'Not around here, was he?'

'It was queer, Dad. He said his father wrote his mother a letter fifteen years ago—and he just got it. His father had just struck a rich mine. His mother has been dead three years, I believe.'

'That letter must have been delayed,' said Flint Harper dryly.

'Orville seems like a nice boy.'

'I suppose,' sighed Flint Harper. 'He didn't tell the boy where that mine was located, did he?'

'Orville did not say whether he did or not.'

'Well,' said Flint Harper quietly, 'queer things do happen.'

'I am beginning to think so, too,' replied Norma quietly.

Flint Harper looked curiously at her as she went up the stairs, but turned back to his moody contemplation of the floor. His pride had been badly hurt by Micky Davis, and he wondered what to do about it.

VI

'Cousin Red'

Micky rode home trying to be sorry about his verbal encounter with Flint Harper, but failed utterly. He was sorry that Norma had heard what was said. It might look to her as though he was trying to incriminate her father in her presence.

He found Spook and Orville together in the ranch house. Sleep had done wonders for Orville, and he seemed in fairly good spirits.

'This here redhead shore tells a queer story,' said Spook, when Micky sat down with them. 'Mebbe I can kinda give you a outline of things. Red goes into too damn many details.'

Spook, with a little help from Orville, gave Micky a résumé of things that had happened since Orville got that fifteen-year-old letter.

'I have only a vague remembrance of my father,' said Orville. 'He went away while I was quite young.'

'When them fellers took you off that stage, did they say anything about why they was doin' it?' asked Micky.

'I don't believe they spoke a word until we arrived at our destination. The kidnaping is as much a mystery to me as it is to you. One of them

75

said to the Mexican, "We may not be back before tomorrow night." Where they were going, I do not know.'

'The stage driver says that you were drunk when you got on the stage at Sierra Vista.'

'Yes, I suppose I was—for the first time in my life.'

'What was the names of the punchers you got drunk with?'

'One was Shorty. I believe one was named Ike, and the other one was a big, bowlegged fellow with whiskers.'

'Shorty Boland, Ike Akers, and Jud Moran,' said Micky. 'They work for the Seven-Up outfit, down on Antelope Flats. We can count them out, 'cause I've known them for years. They're too darned lazy to go to all that trouble to play a joke.'

'He says he was down in a canyon,' remarked Spook.

'I suppose it was,' agreed Orville. 'It was like looking up the sides of very tall buildings at night when there are no lights on.'

'The horse took you out of there, eh?'

'Why, yes. It was a terrible climb, and once I thought the animal was going to fall over backwards. It must have been a very narrow pathway, because several times I nearly had my legs scraped off against the rocks. It was terrible.'

'Where were you when daylight came?' asked Micky.

'Out in those everlasting hills.'

Micky rubbed his chin thoughtfully for a while.

'No use askin' you if you could find that canyon again. Lemme see. They grabbed you at Pancho's Place and took you to a canyon. Spook, they must have taken him to Lobo Solo Canyon.'

'Yeah, I thought of that, too. But if you remember, there ain't no way of gettin' down into the canyon without comin' halfway down the length of the darn thing. There's about twelve miles of that canyon that you can't get down into it 'less you got wings.'

'Yeah, that's true,' agreed Micky. 'She's pretty rough goin' out there. I figure it would take four hours, easy, in the dark to get to where they could get into that canyon. Was you ridin' that long?'

'I believe,' replied Orville soberly, 'I was on that horse for at least a week.'

'I reckon they made Lobo Solo,' said Spook.

'I reckon we better go to bed,' said Micky.

Sunday morning, and the three men at the Bar D slept late. It was after nine o'clock when Micky got up to cook breakfast. Spook went through his usual yawns, snorts, grunts, and curses before getting both feet out of bed.

'Some day,' he told the still snoring Orville, 'I'm goin' to git me a job where I don't have to work in the daytime and can sleep all night.'

No answer from Orville. Spook dressed and went into the kitchen, redolent with odors of ham and eggs, blended with the aroma of coffee.

'Is Red up yet?' asked Micky.

'Up? Hell, that jigger ain't moved. He can sleep louder than I can.'

'You better go down and shovel a little hay to them horses before breakfast,' said Micky. 'It'll give you an appetite.'

'Better jist fry me four aigs,' said Spook. 'I'm kinda peckish today.'

Tilting his hat at a rakish angle, Spook slouched down to the stable. Spook always slouched before breakfast. Micky leaned in the kitchen doorway, dangling a butcher knife in his right hand. Just as Spook entered the stable, Buck Bramer, the sheriff, and Duncan Wheeler rode around the corner and drew up at the kitchen door.

'Howdy, gents?' said Micky.

'All right, Micky,' replied the sheriff. 'How's things with you?'

'Pretty good, I reckon,' said Micky. 'We ain't been up long enough to find out. What's on your mind?'

'That trouble between you and Flint Harper.'

Micky laughed shortly. 'Don't let that get you down. Did Flint make a complaint?'

'I reckon Flint Harper can take care of himself.'

'That's fine, Buck. So can I, and that makes us even. That ought to take a load off your mind.'

'Micky, I don't want to see any trouble. Flint is

one of our big men around here, and last night you openly accused him of bein' a rustler.'

'Do you *know* he isn't, Buck?'

'Why, certainly!'

'If you know so damn much,' said Micky evenly, 'you might tell me who stole my calves.'

'I wouldn't have any way of knowin'.'

'No, and you haven't any way of knowin' that Flint Harper is an honest man.'

The sheriff opened his mouth and started to speak, but was interrupted by a crashing down in the stable. Spook Sullivan leaped through the open door. It was easily a world's record leap, except that the landing was not in good form. Spook crashed against the corral fence, bounced sideways, and went sprawling for a moment or two. Then he got to his feet, staggered around in a circle, then stopped and stood staring at the two riders beside the kitchen doorway.

He started for the kitchen, stopped, and went cautiously back to the stable, where he peered around a corner of the doorway. Slowly he reached back, drew his gun, and fired two shots into the stable. Then he holstered his gun and came back to the kitchen.

'What was it, Spook?' asked Micky.

Spook's face was grim, a frightened expression in his eyes.

'Dad-bub-burned rattler in the stable,' he said. 'Didn't miss me an inch.'

'Did you kill it?' asked the sheriff.

'Na-a-aw. Took a couple shots at it as it was crawlin' down a hole in the floor. H-how are you, Buck?'

'Scared of snakes, eh?' jeered Duncan Wheeler. 'Is there anythin' that you ain't scared of, Spook?'

'I ain't scared of any human bein', Dunc,' replied Spook, and added, 'You might file that away in the back of your mind, in case you're tempted to make a mistake some day.'

'What seems to be the trouble?' asked Orville, poking his red-thatched head outside the door-way. 'Weren't there shots fired?'

'Oh, gosh!' gasped Spook. 'Him!'

'It—it wasn't anythin', Red,' said Micky quickly. 'This is Sheriff Bramer and Duncan Wheeler. Gents, this is—uh—my cousin Red Orville.'

'Howdy,' said the sheriff gravely, but Wheeler merely nodded.

'He's spendin' a few days with me,' explained Micky. 'Red's from the East.'

Orville looked questioningly at Micky, wondering what it was all about. He looked at Spook, whose left eyelid was opening and closing at excessive speed.

'Well!' exclaimed Orville. 'What a lovely morning!'

'You didn't expect rain, did you?' asked Wheeler.

'One never knows, does one?' queried Orville brightly.

'Your face looks like you'd been in a fight,' remarked the sheriff.

'I told him to leave the axe alone,' declared Micky quickly. 'But you know how it is, Buck. Wanted to split wood—and a chunk flew up.'

'Anyway,' said Orville stoutly, 'it doesn't matter to anyone else, because this happens to be my face, you know.'

'That's tellin' 'em, Red,' applauded Spook. 'Let's me and you go ahead and cook that breakfast. I'm hongry.'

'We won't keep you from breakfast,' said the sheriff. 'Just passin', you know. Found any more calves, Micky?'

'No. I reckon they're safe in Mexico.'

'Well, I wouldn't put it past Topete.'

'Not if there was any inducement for him to steal 'em, Buck.'

'I don't reckon he'd need any more inducement than a couple hundred yearlin's. Well, I'll see you later, Micky.'

'*Adios*,' called Micky.

'*Vaya con diablo*,' added Spook soberly.

'I guess I better put on my shirt,' said Orville, and went into the house.

Micky turned quickly to Spook. 'What went wrong with you down there?'

'It's there—in a manger,' said Spook.

'A rattler?'

'No-o-o—that damn skeleton!'

Micky stared at him for several moments. Then he said:

'I reckon I better finish cookin' breakfast.'

Orville wanted to go down to the stable and see the snake, but Spook advised against it.

'I have never seen a live rattler,' said Orville.

'Yuh never have?' queried Spook, slightly aghast. 'Yuh ain't never see *one?*'

'Not one,' declared Orville.

'Then don't go see this'n,' advised Spook soberly. 'I wouldn't want to be responsible for lettin' yuh see yore first one, Red. Yuh never know what the sight may do to yuh.'

'I do not believe I understand, Spook.'

' 'Course yuh don't. Not havin' lived in a rattler country, yuh wouldn't know the awful effects of the first one. Some folks look at their first one jist like you'd look at a piece of rope—as yuh are now—havin' seen ropes.'

Spook was stalling. He did not want Orville to go down there and see that skeleton sitting up in the manger, in plain sight from the front door. Spook looked appealingly at Micky, who was calmly frying bacon, an amused expression on his face, as he listened to Spook.

'Just in what way do they affect one?' queried Orville.

'Oh, terrible—sometimes,' sighed Spook.

'Sometimes jist the sight of one causes people to break out in spots. Fact. I've seen 'em git right down on their belly and crawl. Some of 'em try to coil up, and'—Spook drew a deep breath—'and I've even seen 'em try to *rattle.*'

'Whew!' exclaimed Micky, stepping back from the stove and wiping his eyes. 'Bacon splatters are especially bad today,' he said.

'That's a rattlesnake sign,' declared Spook. 'Any time the bacon splatters—there's a rattler around close.'

'Why would a rattlesnake affect frying bacon?' queried Orville.

'Red,' replied Spook gravely, 'there's a lot of things that none of us know about. It jist is. Mebbe it's like showin' a red rag to a bull.'

'I have heard about that,' admitted Orville.'

'Have yuh?' queried Spook brightly. 'That's fine. Why, I was thirty years of age before I knowed that. Yo're five years ahead of me. Can yuh imagine that, Micky?'

'Sometimes,' replied Micky, 'they learn young.'

'Ain't that a fact?'

'Was it a big rattler?' asked Orville, still clinging to the idea of seeing the reptile.

'Well, I'll tell yuh,' replied Spook. 'He wasn't ext'rordinary in length, but he shore was colossal in thickness. Oh, I'd say he was twelve, fifteen feet long, but what impressed me was his thickness. You've seen beer-kegs, ain't yuh?

Well, yuh could knock both ends out of a beer-keg and this here snake could wear it for a necklace.'

Micky placed breakfast on the table and began pouring coffee.

'I see,' said Orville, but a bit dubiously. 'You said he went down through a hole in the floor, didn't you?'

Spook drew a deep breath and looked at Micky, who blinked at him through misty eyes.

'Oh, shore,' agreed Spook heartily. 'Snakes is elastic. They shrink themselves to almost nothin' in thickness. Stretch. Gosh, you'd be surprised. I'll betcha if he had to that snake could stretch himself fifty feet long, and he wouldn't be any thicker'n a lead-pencil. Ain't that true, Micky?'

'Dig in on them eggs before they get cold,' said Micky hoarsely. 'Some day Red will learn all about rattlers.'

'Yeah, I reckon he will,' agreed Spook. 'They're remarkable.'

'They must be,' agreed Orville. 'Anyway, they *sound* remarkable.'

'Almost unbelievable,' admitted Micky.

'Facts,' said Spook, reaching for the sugar, 'don't lie.'

'Not many of 'em in Arizona,' remarked Micky soberly.

After breakfast, and while Spook lied some more to Orville, Micky went down to the stable, took the skeleton up into the hayloft and buried it under loose hay. Apparently someone had placed it in the stable, where the sheriff might discover it and swear that Micky and Spook had stolen it.

Micky climbed down the ladder and stepped outside. As he did so, a twelve-inch sidewinder, the smallest of the rattlesnakes, came from the corral, traveling in its own peculiar way and heading toward the shade of the stable.

Micky drew his .45, and as the little snake stopped a few feet away, blew its head and several inches of its body away. Picking up its twitching length, he carried it up to the kitchen doorway, where Spook and Orville were waiting curiously.

Spook looked sadly upon the remains.

'What is it?' queried Orville.

'That's what allus happens to a rattler when he's had his head shot off,' said Spook quickly. 'He shrinks to almost nothin'.'

'I see-e-e,' muttered Orville. 'In life he could wear a beer-keg for a necklace.'

'Shore, he could!' snorted Spook. ' 'Course it might be a little awkward to handle.'

Duncan Wheeler and the sheriff rode back to Encinitas, where they met Norma Harper and her father.

'Have you found the missin' young man yet?' asked Flint Harper.

'Not yet,' replied the sheriff. 'You saw him in Sierra Vista, didn't you, Flint?'

'Yeah; he came in on the train with Norma.'

'Is that so! Somebody said his name was Woodruff.'

'His name is Orville Woodruff,' said Norma. Wheeler and the sheriff exchanged knowing glances.

'Orville's a peculiar name,' remarked the sheriff. 'Didja learn anythin' else about him, Norma?'

'No,' answered Norma, 'except that he has very red hair.'

'Well, I expect we'll run across him one of these days. We just came in from Davis's place, Flint.'

'Well?' queried the big cattleman.

'It seems,' replied the sheriff, 'that the young man is goin' to stick with his original statement.'

'I don't reckon we'll discuss that subject on a Sunday mornin',' said Flint Harper stiffly. 'It's a weekday job, Buck.'

Norma went upstairs, and her father followed the sheriff and Duncan Wheeler out on the porch.

'I didn't want to talk about Micky in front of Norma, Buck,' said Harper.

'That's what I figured. Well, he still thinks you stole his calves, Flint. I tried to argue him out of the idea, but yuh can't git no place arguin' with Micky Davis.'

'I found that out,' said Harper dryly. 'I don't want trouble with him, Buck; but a feller can't ignore it entirely when he's openly accused of bein' a rustler.'

'I know it, Flint. Speakin' about that Woodruff feller—he's down at Micky's ranch.'

'He is?'

'Yeah, he is,' smiled the sheriff. 'I dunno what the idea is, but Micky introduced him to me as his cousin, Red Orville. Kinda had me stuck, until Norma said his first name was Orville and that he had red hair.'

'I wonder why he lied to yuh, Buck.'

'Force of habit, I reckon. I wonder how he got lost off the stage, and where he went. His face shows that he's been in a fight, but Micky said he was splittin' wood and a chunk flew up and hit him.'

'Kinda funny,' mused Harper. 'That skeleton's name was Woodruff, too.'

'Sure,' nodded the sheriff. 'And there was that old letter, lost in the post office, directed to Mary Woodruff. The old man sent it on. I didn't ask him how long it had been lost. And here is Orville Woodruff, goin' under the name of Red Orville. Kinda funny, Flint.'

'It all connects up, Buck. Woodruff told Norma that he just got a letter that his father wrote fifteen years ago to his mother. His mother has been dead several years. He told Norma that his father had discovered a rich mine. Mebbe he's lookin' for it.'

'Prob'ly that's why he's here. But I don't remember anybody makin' a rich strike in Smoke Tree Valley. Every prospect has played out. Unless this Woodruff made a rich strike and was killed before it became public.'

'But if he was murdered for his mine, why ain't the killer got a mine? It don't work out, Buck.'

'Yeah, that's right. Mebbe they was tryin' to find him and force him to tell where it was when he crawled into that crevice, and they never found him. That's reasonable, Flint.'

'Well, I'm afraid it's just another ghost mine, Buck. Anyway, I'm a lot more interested in makin' Micky Davis keep his mouth shut.'

'So am I, Flint; I don't want trouble to break out. What was he talkin' about—you influencin' the bank to loan him money?'

'Well, you knew he got a loan from the bank on his ranch, and then he spent the money for Mexican calves. If his calves are lost, he owes the money to the bank—and if he can't pay the bank—'

'They'll take the ranch back again. I see his angle. He thinks you want the Bar D.'

'Well, I wouldn't steal it from him,' declared Harper stiffly.

'Sure yuh wouldn't, Flint. But to a man up a tree it looks like a roundabout way of gettin' yore property back.'

'That's right. Well, I hope Micky finds his calves.'

'I'm afraid they're back in Mexico,' sighed the sheriff.

'So am I, Buck; and I can't prove I didn't pay somebody to take 'em back there.'

'Well,' drawled Wheeler, entering the discussion for the first time, 'I wouldn't worry about Micky Davis, Flint. He talks a lot. Everybody knows you wouldn't pull a crooked deal.'

'Everybody except Micky Davis,' corrected Flint Harper.

Orville Woodruff sat in an old chair on the porch of the Bar D ranch house, humped over, as he examined the rusty old Colt revolver which Micky had found with the skeleton in that crevice. Spook Sullivan sprawled on the steps. Micky Davis sat on the railing, hugging one knee, while he looked soberly at Orville.

'I know just how you feel, Red,' he said quietly. 'I'll be damned if I'd want anybody playin' three-card monte with my old man's remains. But what else could I do? I had to cache 'em. There's a law against stealin' anythin' like that, you know.'

'As a matter of fact,' said Orville, 'there isn't any proof that it *is* the remains of my father. The name scratched on the sandstone doesn't identify anything.'

'I was thinkin' about that,' said Spook. 'It's jest possible that mebbe your father gunned down this poor son of a buck, and he was tryin' to put the deadwood on your father.'

'That is a very pleasant thought, Spook,' said Orville. 'You see, I have only a sketchy remembrance of my father. Naturally, there was no love between us. He was just a name. This may have been his gun. I am very glad to have it. As far as those samples of ore are concerned—I wouldn't know gold from brass.'

'We never went in very heavy on brass mines around here,' said Spook. 'I don't reckon it's plentiful at all.'

'Some of these days we'll clean up that old gun for you,' said Micky. 'It'll prob'ly work all right.'

'I have never fired a gun,' said Orville.

'Never have? Well, far be it from me to teach you any bad habits; but after what happened to you the other night, you ought to get a gun and learn to shoot. It might help you out some-time.'

'You mean—carry a gun like you and Spook?'

'Why not?'

'I might shoot myself.'

'We might, too,' grinned Spook. 'That's a chance we all have to take here in Arizony, Red.

You git a gun, and we'll learn you how to keep the muzzle away from your anatomy.'

'But I couldn't shoot a man,' protested Orville.

'That's what *I* thought when I came here,' said Spook soberly. 'The first one was kinda hard—seein' him kickin' around in the dirt. But, shucks, I got so used to it that I never even gave 'em a second look.'

Orville looked in amazement at this hardened killer. 'I—I didn't know you—killed so many,' he said.

'There's a can out behind the kitchen where he keeps the rattles,' informed Micky.

'Rattles? Why, I was speaking about shooting men.'

'O-o-oh!' drawled Spook. 'I reckon I'm gettin' kinda hard of hearin'. I jest happened to think about an old Colt .45 I've got. We'll clean her up, and you can learn with it, Red.'

'You can't hit anythin' with that old cannon,' said Micky.

'I know I can't—but mebbe he can. C'mon, pupil; teacher's got an example that's got to be worked.'

Spook secured the old .45, an assortment of rags, hot water, and some kerosene, after which he and Orville sat in the shade on the kitchen steps and proceeded to put the old sixshooter in shape for some shooting lessons.

'Orville, this here gun ain't much to look upon,

but she's one killer, if yuh ask me. 'Course, after a while you'll be like the rest of us gun-fighters. You'll want a gun with silver doodads, fancy sights, and all that kinda stuff. It allus happens after yuh kill three-four men and yuh start gettin' proud.

'I member my first killin'. I had an old hog-l aig, rusty—why, when I cocked it yuh could hear that cylinder creak a hundred yards away. Wasn't no sights on it either. Hm-m-m-m. That shore was a *gun!*'

'Did you shoot his head off?' queried Orville.

'Whose head?'

'The snake's head.'

'Oh!'

Spook scrubbed violently at the rusty barrel.

'Yuh never heard about the duel me and Billy the Kid fought, didja?' asked Spook.

'Who was Billy the Kid?'

'Then *that* ain't any good,' sighed Spook. 'Well, I dunno.'

He replaced the cylinder, squirted on some oil, and began cocking and snapping the old weapon. Satisfied that it would function properly, he loaded five of the six chambers.

'That's how yuh load it, Orville,' he drawled. 'Yuh see how to do it, don'tcha?'

'Is there any other way you might load it, Spook?'

'No, I don't guess yuh can make any mistake

and load it wrong. Now, we're goin' to learn the first lesson. C'mon out back of the barn, where a stray bullet can pick its part of Arizona as a permanent residence.'

They went behind the barn, where Spook picked up a tin can. Handing the gun to Orville he started to walk away, but came back and took the gun from Orville's hand.

'Teacher's cautious,' he said quietly. 'Teacher don't like bullets in his back.'

Walking out about twenty feet he placed the can on the ground, came back, and handed the gun to Orville.

'The idea of this here proceedin's, Orville,' he explained, 'is to cock the gun, take deadly aim at that can, gently but firmly squeeze the trigger, and hit the can. It's simple. The gun'll make a big boom when she goes off, but you'll hear it jist as loud with yore eyes open as yuh will with 'em closed, so yuh might as well keep 'em open. In case yuh shoot a man, you'll want to see his death agony.

'That's right. Hook yore thumb over that hammer and haul her back—all the way back! Oh-h-h-h-h!'

Orville failed to cock the old single-action gun fully, the hammer snapped down, and the big gun went off, tearing a hole in the gravel close to Orville's right foot. Orville, slightly pale, stared at Spook.

'What—what did I do wrong?' he gasped.

'Everythin',' replied Spook fearfully. 'Yuh let that hammer slip.'

'Did I?'

'Did yuh? I hope to tell yuh. Here—let me show yuh.'

Spook carefully cocked the weapon, got directly behind Orville, and shoved the gun past his right elbow.

'Take it in yore right hand, Orville. That's right. Keep the muzzle straight out. The muzzle is the hell-bendin' end of the gun, in case yo're confused. That's right. Now point it at the can. Fine. Look over the top of the barrel, line up them sights, and squeeze.'

Orville breathless, his right hand wobbling in circles, reared back, his knuckles white from gripping the heavy gun.

'Well, why in hell don'tcha shoot?' whispered Spook.

'I—I'm squeezing,' whispered Orville tensely. Another ten seconds of wobbling muzzle, and Spook said huskily:

'Jist what in hell are yuh squeezin', Orville?'

'The gug-gun.'

'Oh, my!' gasped Spook. 'You've been tryin' to pull off the trigger-guard, Orville. Pull the trigger. It's that projection back of where you've been pullin'.'

Wham! Orville discovered it, and the bullet tore

a six-inch gash in the dirt twelve feet short of the can. Spook mopped his steaming face with his shirtsleeve and leaned back against the stable.

'Well, that was better,' said Spook. 'It missed us about eight feet that time. You keep improvin' all the time. Try it again.'

'Personally,' said Orville, 'I doubt that I shall ever become an expert with a revolver.'

'Well,' remarked Spook dryly, 'none of us ever git too good. But most of us git good enough so we ain't a menace to ourselves every time we pull out a gun. With enough practice I believe you'll learn to keep the muzzle of the gun away from yuh when yuh shoot. Try that can again. Want me to cock it for yuh?'

'No, thanks. I believe I understand the mechanics now.'

'Now! You cocked that fine, Orville. Don't point it down! My, my, you can't afford to sacrifice yore toes. Lemme tell yuh somethin'. Some shooters elevate the muzzle above the target, lower it slowly, and shoot when it comes in line. Others point below the target, lift the muzzle to the target, and let her go. Pick yore style, feller.'

'I—I believe I prefer the former, if you do not mind,' said Orville, lifting the muzzle straight up. Tensing his arm, he started to lower the muzzle, but at an angle of forty-five degrees he put too much pressure on the trigger and the .45 roared and bucked.

Spook reached over, took the gun from Orville's unresisting fingers, and drew him back under the eaves of the stable. Spook was staring out toward the horizon, and he held that pose for at least thirty seconds. Orville stared with him, although he did not know what Spook was looking for.

Finally the cowboy drew a deep breath of relief, looked at the old gun, and put it in his pocket.

'What happened?' queried Orville nervously.

'Not a thing. You done well. With only three shots you learned how to make yore gun safe. I'm shore proud of yuh, Orville.'

'Well, th—thank you, Spook. I'm glad I pleased you. But what were you watching for out there?'

'Angels.'

'Angels?' Orville stared at Spook. 'I don't understand.'

'You shootin' in the air thataway,' explained Spook, 'often hits one. Mebbe the flight was a little high today—but I wanted to be sure.'

'Angels? Why, Spook, that is ridiculous.'

'I know it is, but what can yuh do if they insist on flyin' so low over Arizona? The law can't handle things like that, so we just have to be careful. I 'member one day a feller got drunk, shot his six-gun straight up in the air, and got three of 'em. They allus called him "Pot-Shot" after that. He hated it awful. Well, I reckon it's about time to put on a pot of beans.'

'You mean to say he shot three angels, Spook?'

'Angels? No, I was talkin' about crows.'

'I find you are a very disconcerting person, Spook.'

'I'll have to find out what that means before I can answer yuh,' grinned Spook. 'Don't say anythin' to Micky about how good yuh are with the six-gun; he's jealous.'

'Oh, I won't mention it,' assured Orville. 'I—I just wondered if you could tell me something about Miss Norma Harper.'

'Shore,' nodded Spook patronizingly. 'Why, I've knowed her since she was knee-high to a nail. Anythin' yuh want to know, Red.'

'Is Micky in love with her?' asked Orville.

'Is Micky—wait a minute! Are you?'

'Well,' said Orville, 'I wasn't sure about—er—prior rights, you know. I wouldn't want to—well, after all, I admire Micky.'

'I see. You didn't happen to mention the condition of yore heart while you and her was on that train, didja?'

'You mean—my admiration for her? Oh, not at all. But under the circumstances—Micky having a girl in Mexico, you know.'

'Oh-h-h-h-h!' breathed Spook. 'He has, eh? Well, I don't reckon Micky would mind havin' yuh relocate his claim. After all, Micky can't expect to file a claim on every eligible female. He's got to let somebody else have a chance. Yo're a nice boy. No, I don't reckon he'd care if yuh made love to Norma. 'Course you'd have to git her consent.'

'Oh, I realize that, Spook. You have relieved my mind, I assure you.'

'Well, you've done taken quite a load off mine, too, Red. Now we'll cook the beans. Don't say anythin' to Micky about Norma.'

'Naturally not.'

The next morning Orville made his first trip to Encinitas. Micky had outfitted him with a gentle horse and one of their extra saddles, and inside his waistband reposed an old .45 Colt, which was a very uncomfortable encumbrance to Orville Woodruff. Micky and Spook were taking a long ride along Lobo Solo Canyon; too long, they decided, for an inexperienced rider. Orville wanted to make a few purchases and then return to the ranch. He needed more cartridges for his sixshooter.

Encinitas folks looked curiously at him because of his lack of tan and because he was a stranger; but he proceeded to purchase a Stetson hat, a pair of high-heeled boots, and plenty of ammunition. He immediately donned the hat and boots, and furnished amusement to the people in the store when he walked out. The cowboy boot, with its underset high heel, is a tricky article of footwear and requires considerable practice.

He went into the post office to purchase some stamps.

'You don't happen to be going out to Harper's ranch, do you?' asked the old postmaster. 'Reason I asked is 'cause I've got one of them special delivery letters for Norma Harper, and I ain't got no way to send it.'

'Why, yes,' said Orville. 'I'll take it out there.'

From a man outside the post office he got directions to the Harper ranch. He tied his packages on the saddle, mounted, and rode out of town, rather thrilled at being able to do a favor for Norma Harper.

'I dunno who the hell he is,' remarked a cowboy standing with a group in the doorway of a saloon, as Orville rode away, 'but he wears his gun inside his waistband, and he's got red hair. Them is two handicaps I ain't never been able to overcome.'

'Looks to me like a damn dude,' remarked a gambler.

'Well, mebbe he is, but I ain't never seen no dude wearin' his six-gun inside the waist of his pants. If you want to play with him, don't let me hinder you none.'

Unaware that he had made any impression in Encinitas, Orville rode slowly along on his way to the Harper ranch. His heart beat high with the hope that he would get a chance to see Norma again, and do her the favor of bringing a letter.

The big hat felt clumsy on his head, and his toes ached from the tight boots. Every time the horse trotted the hat joggled from side to side, and that big sixshooter added to his discomfort, until he was inclined to tie it to the saddle, but thought better of that.

The road was ankle-deep in hot dust, which kept floating into his eyes, nose, and ears, but he mopped his face with a handkerchief and wondered what Henry Ellis and Joe Buerman would think if they could see him now. Henry Ellis would likely pale at sight of that big gun, which was slowly grinding his middle to a pulp.

Orville took the gun out and pointed it at imaginary foes, and nearly got dumped in the road when the old horse swerved and stopped. Orville did not know that the horse was gun-broke and did not care to have a bullet past its ears. But he put the gun back and went on.

Orville had no fear of being kidnaped again. In fact, he could see no reason for the first kidnaping. It had been a mighty uncomfortable experience, and he did not care to have it happen again. The battle with the Mexican in the cave had done much to encourage Orville's respect for his own physical ability, but so far had not exaggerated
his ego to any extent.

The old ranch buildings of the Circle H were hidden away in a huge grove of sycamores and oaks, a picturesque spot. The main ranch building was two-storied, with roses in the front yard, a large, thick-walled patio at the rear, and a huge arched gate of weathered oak and wrought iron.

There was no one in sight around the ranch as Orville rode in. Slowly he circled around to the patio gate, where he saw a beautiful horse tied to a ring in the wall, the sunlight flashing back from the silver-trimmed saddle.

Without any hesitation Orville rode in beside the horse, dismounted clumsily, and tied his horse to the same ring. As he stepped toward the gate he distinctly heard Norma's voice. Then he stepped into the open gateway.

VII

An Error

Miguel Topete was a huge Mexican of ample girth, gaudy raiment, and heavy mustache. He was as vain as a peacock, egotistical, and altogether ruthless in his actions. Ignorance plus his exalted opinion of himself made him a sort of leader in his own little district. In a way he was a semi-bandit, resorting to outside-the-law endeavors in order to make a little extra cash.

Today he rode to the Circle H ranch to talk sales of cattle to Flint Harper. Topete wore a red shirt with silver buttons, a sea-green muffler, and on his huge head a cream-colored sombrero surmounted with a silver band.

His black broadcloth pants, as tight-fitting as the skin on a sausage, were worn inside gaudy high-heeled boots, and the rowels of his silver Mexican spurs had the circumference of a saucer. He rode a palomino gelding, sitting haughtily in a silver-trimmed saddle, his silver bit chains jingling as he rode up to the ranch.

Topete never made appointments. Not seeing anyone around the ranch house, he jingled his spurs into the patio, where Norma was curled up on a leather divan, reading a book. Norma and Sing Low, the Chinese cook, were the only persons at the ranch.

The patio at the Circle H was spacious, surrounded by a thick adobe wall, almost covered with climbing roses. In the center was an old well with a low stone curbing. The floor was of ancient tile, well worn by many feet.

At sight of Miguel Topete, Norma sat up quickly. She had not seen him for several years, but remembered who he was. Topete scowled at her, then smiled broadly and twisted his mustache.

'*Por Dios*!' he muttered. 'Theese leetle señorita ees grown up to beautee-ful woman.'

'Mr. Topete, I—I haven't seen you for a long time.'

'You remember me, eh? That ees fine. W'ere ees your papa?'

'He and the boys went out on the north range.'

'Oh, I am ver' sorry. They weel not be home until late?'

'Some time this afternoon, Mr. Topete.'

'Hm-m-m!' Topete caressed his mustache. 'Per'aps there ees one of the boys around that I can talk weeth.'

'Only myself and Sing Low. Perhaps tomorrow—'

'It ees not important,' he assured her. 'W'at ees the use of talk business, w'en there ees the cool shade, a beautiful señorita, roses—' Topete gestured airily, his little piglike eyes considering Norma carefully.

'I am sorry, Mr. Topete,' said Norma, getting to her feet. 'If you wish to see my father—come tomorrow.'

Topete smiled at her, a calculating expression in his eyes.

'Tomorrow ees a long time, *dulce amiga.*'

Sweetheart! Norma flushed hotly. Topete was between her and the doorway. No use calling for help. Sing Low, a little old Chinaman, would be no help in a case of this kind. Topete was swaying toward her, laughing deep in his thick throat.

'You touch me, and my father will kill you,' she said.

'Your father ees not 'ere,' he told her.

'You think he wouldn't come after you?'

'Tomorrow, next day Topete has sold out—everytheeng. Vamose—who knows where? Today I am 'ere—tomorrow—*quién sabe*?'

Norma had not lost her nerve. If she could get into the house, lock the door, she would be safe. There were plenty of weapons in the house, and she knew how to use them. Summoning up her nerve, she looked past him, widened her eyes, and said:

'Look out!'

Topete whirled, his right hand jerking at his holstered gun. Norma sprang past him, but tripped on a loose tile, and Topete whirled around, grasping her sleeve.

'You leetle devil!' he panted. 'You try to fool Topete. Come—I geeve you a keess for that.'

He grasped her arms roughly with both hands, and was drawing her close to him, when a voice behind him said:

'I'm sorry, but—'

Topete jerked away from her, and Norma almost fell to her knees. It was Orville Woodruff, standing only a few feet away, the letter in his hand. Norma, white-faced and panting heavily, stared at him. He did not seem to notice anything incongruous in the situation.

'Here is a letter for you,' he said to Norma, and walked over to deliver it, ignoring Topete.

Suddenly, the big Mexican lashed out with a brawny fist. The blow landed solidly on Orville's right ear, knocking him flat on his face, almost against the porch. Norma tried again to take advantage of the situation, but Topete flung her aside, tearing a sleeve from her waist. She staggered against the old divan, barely holding her balance.

For the moment Topete ignored Orville, who sat up, dazed, his ear bleeding, but with that old sixshooter in his hand. Norma's scream was echoed by the heavy report of the .45. Topete's feet seemed to have been yanked from under him, and he came down with a crash, striking his head on the curbing of the well.

Orville got slowly to his feet, staring at the huddled figure of Miguel Topete. Blood was trickling from Topete's nose and temple, and the skin of his face looked like dirty putty.

Norma, leaning back against the divan, said weakly: 'I—I think you've killed him.'

Orville stared at her, his eyes wide. Then he shifted his eyes and looked at Topete.

'Killed him?' he whispered. 'Killed him? God help me!'

With the gun gripped in his right hand, Orville looked wildly around, then darted for the gateway of the patio, galloping insecurely on his high heels. Perhaps he was still dazed from Topete's blow. To his whirling mind, a horse was only a horse, and he rode away from the Circle H ranch unaware of the fact that he was sitting in a silver-trimmed saddle, and that the running horse beneath him was a palomino gelding. Previous to this, even a short, slow gallop was an experience; but now he stood in his stirrups and whipped the palomino with his new Stetson, while his red hair blew straight up in the wind, the sixshooter clenched in his good right hand.

Nor did Orville slow down for Encinitas. Straight down the main street he went, running the palomino at top speed, and leaving a cloud of dust behind him. People ran into the street behind him, watching him disappear in the distance.

'That's *him* again!' yelled the cowboy who had remarked about the way Orville carried his gun. 'He's done traded horses, and the way he's ridin', wavin' his gun, I'll betcha his back trail is soggy with dead men.'

Norma, sick and frightened over the affair, went into the house and locked the doors, peering through a window into the patio. Gradually Miguel Topete came to life. He pulled himself to a sitting position, where he sat and held his head for a long time.

After a while he managed to get to his feet, but was very unsteady. His face and neck were covered with blood. He seemed to be making an examination of himself, looking for possible bullet holes. Finally he sat down on the well curb and looked at the heel of his right boot, where the .45 bullet had struck, knocking his feet from under him.

Walking drunkenly, Topete left the patio only to find that his horse was gone. He circled the house and came back to the gateway, where Orville's horse stood. Realizing the necessity of getting away from the Circle H, he mounted Orville's horse and rode away at a jerky gallop.

Instead of searching the upper end of Lobo Solo Canyon that morning, Micky and Spook decided to go into Mexico and have another talk with

Grandma Ramirez. They wanted to know if she learned anything from Manuel, her son. But Manuel had not been home.

The old lady did not seem greatly concerned over Manuel's absence, as he often stayed a week or longer.

'I jest wonder if Orville cooled off that Manuel in the canyon,' said Spook, as they rode back to the border. 'It might be that Mr. Manuel got himself a harp. Orville said he was shore out cold when he left there that night.'

'Well, I ain't goin' to take down my hair and start weepin',' declared Micky. 'Manuel's no good—dead or alive.'

They were about a mile north of the border, traveling along a narrow trail, when they came face to face with Miguel Topete, riding on Orville's horse. The big Mexican was swaying drunkenly in the saddle as Micky spurred in close, the muzzle of his gun almost against Topete's body. Quickly, Micky reached over and removed Topete's gun from his holster.

'Looks like he'd been in a battle,' said Spook grimly.

'Ridin' a stolen horse,' gritted Micky. 'What have you got to say for yourself, you penny-ante bandit?'

'*No comprender*,' replied Topete huskily.

'Where'd you steal that horse and saddle?'

'*No comprender*. I theenk I am seek.'

'Yeah, and you'll be a hell of a lot sicker before we get through with you. Gimme them reins; you're goin' to Encinitas. Spook, you ride behind him. If he makes a crooked move, sock him with a bullet right between the shoulders. He's pretty thick there, so it won't come through and hit me.'

'I'll sock him,' promised Spook. 'In fact, I hope he makes a crooked move.'

But Topete was too sick to make any crooked moves. They took him straight to the sheriff's office, where Skee Harris looked them over critically.

'Throw this horse thief in a good, strong cell, Skee,' said Micky. 'I charge him with stealin' the horse and saddle he's sittin' on.'

'Got anythin' to say for yourself, Topete?' asked Harris.

'*No comprender*,' mumbled Topete.

'You kinda banged him up, didn't you?' remarked the deputy.

'He was that way when we found him. Mebbe he needs a doctor.'

'I'll have Doc Mitchell take a squint at him,' promised Skee. They helped Topete off the horse and watched the deputy lock him in a cell. Afterward, they told Skee that Orville had left Micky's place on the horse that they found Topete riding.

'What the hell do you reckon happened to this

Orville gent?' asked Skee. 'This Mexican mebbe killed him.'

'Yeah—he might,' admitted Micky. 'It's shore all mixed up. We don't even know where to look for this tenderfoot. I reckon we'll go out to the ranch and take a look.'

'I'll tell Buck as soon as he shows up,' promised Skee.

Micky and Spook lost no time in riding out to the ranch. There was a saddled horse at the kitchen door—Topete's palomino.

'What in the hell!' snorted Micky as they swung down.

They banged into the house and found Orville sitting in the main room. His right ear was swollen and inflamed; his red hair stood on end; his eyes were full of fright.

'I've killed a man,' he said.

'You did, huh?' replied Micky calmly.

'I reckon that practice helped quite a lot,' remarked Spook.

'I tell you I killed him,' insisted Orville. 'I shot him down.'

'You hardly ever see one go up,' said Spook.

'Won't you be sensible?' wailed Orville. 'I am nearly crazy.'

'Askin' people to be somethin' that you ain't. Who'd you shoot?'

'I don't know,' wailed Orville.

'That makes it fine,' remarked Micky. 'After

thirty minutes' target practice, you go right out and shoot somebody that you don't even know. Would you mind tellin' us how and why you did it?'

Trying to be calm in his narrative, Orville told them about the letter and his offer to deliver it to Norma Harper. He told about arriving at the ranch, finding no one, and entering the patio. There he beheld Norma Harper in the arms of a man.

'They—they fell apart as I spoke,' he said. 'I gave Norma the letter, and this man struck me on the ear, knocking me down. I—I suppose I lost my head. In my dazed condition I heard her scream; so I—well, I shot him down.'

Micky and Spook looked curiously at each other. Things were beginning to clear up a little.

'A big man, wearin' fancy clothes?' asked Micky.

'Yes, I believe he was,' nodded Orville miserably.

'Mebbe that was his horse you rode home,' suggested Spook.

'I don't know,' wailed Orville. 'I was so upset that I really don't know what horse I rode home.'

'I reckon you got the best of the trade,' said Micky.

'What trade?'

'Well, we won't discuss that part of it. Wait a minute!' Micky's voice changed suddenly. 'You say he had Norma in his arms?'

'Yes, he did.'

'Miguel Topete allus was a great lover,' remarked Spook.

'Shut up!' snapped Micky. 'There wasn't anybody home except Norma. Topete came there—yea-a-ah!' Micky's eyes narrowed. 'Orville, are you sure that this big man wasn't just holdin' her?'

'There are only two incidents which stand out in my mind,' replied Orville miserably. 'One is the fact that he knocked me down, and the other is that I killed him. Now what am I going to do?'

'Stand your ground,' advised Spook. 'You ain't a bad shot. You'd go down in hist'ry as Orville the Kid. In my opinion, you're the logical successor to Billy the Kid.'

'Aw, let up on him, Spook,' said Micky. 'He's suffered enough. You didn't kill anybody, Orville. I dunno what happened to him, but me and Spook found him down near the border, ridin' your horse. We turned him over to the law, and he's in jail at Encinitas.'

'You did?' gasped Orville. 'Why—Oh, no, it can't be the same man. I saw him—and I know a dead man when I see one.'

'He insists on bein' a killer, Micky,' sighed Spook. 'It must be in his blood. Just a-honin' for a notch on the handle of his gun, the bloodthirsty critter.'

'Wait a minute, Orville,' said Micky. 'You *didn't* kill anybody. Nobody would blame you if you had—but you did not. Tomorrow we'll go to Encinitas and take a look at this feller—

but I know he's the feller you think you shot.'

'I don't guess he stole Orville's horse,' grinned Spook. 'It was a case of Orville leavin' first.'

'I've got a hunch,' said Micky, 'that he'll wish it was only horse-stealin' when Flint Harper gets hold of him.'

'What would Mr. Harper do?' queried Orville.

'He'd jist about unravel him,' replied Spook.

'How—how could he do that—unravel him, Spook?'

'Didn't yuh ever see that done, Red? Well, sir, it *is* quite a trick. Yuh start out right in the middle of a feller's neck. This here thing that they calls a Adam's apple. Shucks, all that is is the knot they tied when yuh was first knitted.

'Well, they slit that lump, yank out the loose end and start pullin'. Well, sir, it's a caution to cats how yuh unravel. Jist like a knitted sock. If yo're ever around where it's goin' on, you ask the man for the string. There's miles of it, all the same thickness, and when it's braided you've shore got a slick rope. I used one for years. It was originally off a Swede bandit in Sonora, so they told me, but I had m' doubts, 'cause the hair that growed on it was very dark. Mebbe it was the Mexican influence—I dunno.'

Orville stared at Spook for several moments, and turned to Micky.

'Have you ever seen such a rope, Micky?' he asked.

113

'Not one that growed hair,' replied Micky. 'I've seen bald ones.'

'I have never heard of such a thing. Is that what they call flaying a body?'

'Yeah, it is,' agreed Spook quickly. 'It's too bad yuh didn't kill Topete. Man, what a rope his hide would make! Dark in color, but awful tough.'

'Such a thing makes me shudder,' said Orville. 'It was bad enough to have a feeling that I had killed a man. Why, it was horrible. All the way home I rode in the shadow of the gallows.'

'A mighty long gallows,' said Micky soberly.

'Or a hell of a fast one,' added Spook. 'I'll bet that's the first time anybody ever got the best of Topete in a horse trade, Micky.'

'That's right,' nodded Micky, and then to Orville:

'Just what did Norma say when you showed up in the patio?'

'Well, not much,' replied Orville. 'I handed her the letter, then Topete hit me. After I—I shot him, I heard her say, "I think you have killed him."'

'Did—did she say it—like she was sorry for him?'

Orville smiled wearily. 'I am afraid that the tone of voice did not register with me; I was too stunned. I know I got to my feet and looked at his queer-colored face, and I remember saying "God help me!"—and then I—I came home.'

'Well,' remarked Spook quietly, 'I reckon yore prayers was answered in the shape of a palomino —and a live man instead of a dead one. I reckon yore prayers have more muzzle velocity than mine. I'll bet that if yuh could sift 'em out, you'd find all of mine up there about a hundred feet, jist floatin' around. My old dad used to say to me, "Spookie"—he allus called me Spookie for short, m' name bein' Alwin—"Spookie, if there's anythin' yuh want, go and git it—but if yuh start prayin'—keep an eye peeled." My grandfather was prayin' for dry weather when the Johnstown flood hit him.'

'I suppose he was unable to swim,' suggested Orville.

'I dunno about that. They said he was down on his knees when the water sneaked up behind him. Mebbe he never thought to swim, him bein' sorta concentrated on his prayers.'

'I think we better go to bed,' said Micky.

'Was your grandfather named Sullivan, too?' asked Orville.

'Shore. Johnstown Sullivan. They named him after the flood.'

'*After* the flood?' queried Orville. 'Why, I thought—'

'They *had* to. They couldn't name him *before* the flood, when they didn't know there was goin' to be one. Let's go to bed and stop all this foolish argument. I hate it.'

VIII

Four Empty Cells

Micky Davis was correct in his surmise that Flint Harper's reactions would not be friendly toward Miguel Topete. It was nearly dark when Flint Harper and his five cowboys came back to the ranch. Norma told her father what had happened at the ranch that day.

Flint Harper waited until his men finished supper, then he led them outside, told them what had happened, and said:

'This is between me and Topete, boys. I'm not *orderin'* any of you to go along.'

Ten minutes later, six riders left the Circle H, heading south. They avoided Encinitas, avoided Mesquite, and rode straight to Topete's ranch house, a huddle of adobe buildings in a sycamore grove three miles south of the border.

Five Mexicans yelped with fright when the cowboys, headed by Flint Harper, crashed the door of the ranch house. The Mexicans were playing *ecarté* by candlelight, and they sat there like frightened animals as the cowboys crowded into the smoke-filled room. Pete Ortez, one of the men, was Topete's *segundo*, and spoke a fair brand of English.

'Where's Topete?' asked Flint Harper.

'Topete go see you today,' replied Pete, puzzled by the invasion of the cowboys.

'How long has he been back?' queried Harper.

'Topete not come back,' replied Pete.

'You're a liar,' snarled Harper, shoving the muzzle of his gun against the throat of the Mexican.

'I am spik of only w'at I know personally,' stated Pete. 'Topete go see you. Eef he come back—I not see heem.'

Flint Harper looked keenly at the frightened faces of the other Mexicans before turning to his men.

'We'll wait here until he does come. That bug-headed tenderfoot ran away with Topete's palomino, and it may be that Topete is going to get that horse before comin' back. We'll post a guard outside, so we'll spot him before he knows we're here.'

'W'at ees wrong weeth Topete?' asked Pete Ortez.

'His neck's too damn short,' replied a cowboy meaningly.

'Meester 'Arper,' said Pete sorrowfully, 'w'at 'appen to you?'

'Nothin' happened to me,' growled Harper. 'But somethin' is shore goin' to happen to Topete when he comes back.'

'*Dios mio!*'

117

Flint Harper posted his guards and came back into the house.

'Theese Topete do sometheeng?' queried Pete.

'Yeah!' spat Harper. 'And somethin' is goin' to happen to all you *hombres* if yuh don't stop stealin' cattle across the Border.'

'You theenk we are rostlers?' queried Pete. '*Por Dios*—no! Look! I cross my heart and hope you die.'

'All right. But you fellers raided Micky Davis's calf herd.'

'No,' denied Pete. 'Micky Davis ees *amigo* weeth us.'

'You fellers would steal from a friend,' declared a cowboy.

'No,' denied Pete stoutly. 'We are not *Americano*.'

'I reckon that'll hold us for a while,' laughed Ted Byers, one of Harper's cowboys. 'At that, he may be right.'

Flint Harper turned to Ortez. 'Pete, why did Topete come to my ranch today?'

'He theenk he sell you some calf.'

'Sell me some calves, eh?'

'Sure. He like sell some cow, too.'

'What's he tryin' to do—sell out?'

'Sure. He theenk theese cow no good for make money.'

'What's he aimin' to do—turn bandit again?'

'He never tell me. He say theese countree too damn quiet. What he do wrong today?'

'Wait'll he comes—you'll hear all about it—before he stretches a rope.'

'You goin' hang heem?'

'Right on the first tree we can find.'

To Skee Harris there was little importance in the capture of Topete. Of course if Topete had killed the tenderfoot, that might be a different thing. Skee had known the Mexican a long time, but had always considered him petty rather than dangerous. However, he realized that Topete needed medical attention, so he went down to get Doctor Mitchell to attend him.

Topete looked narrowly at the old doctor, but did not explain how he got hurt. He mumbled in Mexican while the doctor took four stitches in the broken scalp and bandaged him carefully.

'Horse kick yuh, Topete?' queried Skee.

'I do' know,' mumbled Topete.

'Somebody hit yuh with a gun?'

Topete scowled thoughtfully. 'I'm theenk I do' know damn theeng.'

'Oh, I see; yo're keepin' it secret. Did the tenderfoot hit yuh?'

'Tanderfoot? What ees that?'

'I guess he didn't. Doc, do yuh reckon he's got concussion?'

'Hardly,' replied the old range doctor. 'In order to have a concussion, you must have brains. He may have a fracture.'

'Mebbe that's what I meant, Doc. Would that make him loco?'

'I don't believe you'd notice it, Skee.'

'Likely not. Micky and Spook caught him on a stolen horse. It was the horse that the tenderfoot—wait a minute! One of the boys was sayin' that he seen the tenderfoot ridin' like hell through town on a palomino. Topete rides a palomino. Topete, did you trade horses with a feller today?'

'No trade 'orse,' declared Topete, feeling of his bandaged head.

'That's out,' sighed Skee. 'Why don't yuh say somethin', Topete?'

'I'm say notheeng,' declared Topete stubbornly.

'Mebbe yo're smarter than I thought.'

'Damn smart,' agreed Topete.

'Well, don't let yore head swell too much,' advised Skee. 'It may leak out the cracks.'

'I'll look him over in the morning, Skee,' promised the doctor. 'I guess he'll live.'

Skee gave Topete some fresh water and locked the door of the cell.

'You goin' keep me here?' queried Topete.

'I hope so,' replied Skee. ' 'Course, if yuh can find a way out it's all right with me—but it won't be through the door.'

'I'm wan' go *Mejico*,' said Topete.

'I'll bet yuh do, feller. But that's nothin' new. Every horse thief we catch has the same yearnin'. *Buenas noches.*'

Skee locked the office and went over to the Smoke Tree Saloon, where he found the cowboy who had told about seeing Orville ride through town on a palomino.

'Didja ever see that palomino that Topete rides?' queried Skee.

'I never paid any attention, Skee.'

'Then yuh wouldn't know if that tenderfoot was ridin' the same horse or not, eh?'

'I'll tell yuh, Skee, I wouldn't. Sweat and dust kinda daub up a horse, and when said horse is goin' like a bat outa hell, how could yuh identify it? Anyway, the head and tail looked palomino.'

'Yo're sure it was the tenderfoot, ain't yuh?'

'If you say he's a tenderfoot—yeah. But that rooster was ridin' like an old rannaham, if yuh ask me. It was the same hombre what rode out of here wearin' a fo'ty-five inside the waistband of his pants. Mebbe that's what fooled me. But the horse he was ridin' shore didn't look palomino—not even the head and tail.'

Skee thanked him for the information, and got into a poker game. Skee loved draw poker. In fact, he loved it so much that he forgot to mention that he had a prisoner in jail. It was past midnight when the last of Skee's wealth disappeared, and he yawned widely.

'No use impoverishin' m'self,' he declared. 'By usin' a lot of willpower, mebbe I can eat until pay day. Deal me out, gents; this game is too long for a shorthorn like me. Gosh, I done forgot to feed my horse!'

'After seein' that bronc you ride,' remarked a cowboy, 'I'll betcha it's a habit with you—forgettin' to feed him. If I had him, I'd cut him off at the shoulders and hips and use him for an accor-deen.'

'He's a little ga'nt,' admitted Skee, 'but he's hard as nails.'

'Yuh can't expect him to be springy on a handful of straw a day.'

Skee laughed, accepted a drink on the house, and went back to the office. But instead of going inside he merely reached for the knob. The door opened ahead of his hand, and something crashed down on his head, knocking him flat on the rickety sidewalk.

He was barely conscious of someone's picking him up and dragging him around to the stable, where he passed out entirely.

When Micky, Spook, and Orville came to Encinitas next morning, Sheriff Buck Bramer was asleep on a cot in his office. Clad only in his underclothes, Buck admitted them, yawning, his eyes full of sleep, but with a certain curiosity about their early morning call.

'We want to take a look at Topete,' said Micky. The sheriff squinted at Micky closely.

'You want to take a look at Topete? I don't sabe.'

'What time did you git home last night, Buck?'

'Oh, about two o'clock. I was up at Sierra Vista.'

'Then you ain't seen Skee Harris?'

'Not since early yesterday mornin', Micky.'

'Well, that accounts for it. You've got Topete in jail—and don't know it. We brought him here, chargin' him with stealin' a horse and saddle.'

'Shucks, I didn't know that! Huh! Shore, you can look at him. I'd kinda like a look at him myself. C'mon.'

The sheriff unlocked the corridor door and led them down between the four individual cells, where they stood in a group, peering into four empty cells.

'It seems to me,' drawled Spook, 'that you'd have to have a hell of a strong imagination to see Topete in this jail.'

The sheriff tested all four doors and found them locked. He looked curiously at Micky, as he rubbed the palm of his right hand across his stubbled chin.

'You wasn't jokin' with me, was you, Micky?' he asked.

'We seen him locked in here, Buck. Mebbe Skee will know what it is all about.'

They walked back into the office, where they

met Doctor Mitchell carrying his little black bag.

'I had to leave town early, so I came to take a look at your prisoner before I left,' he told the sheriff.

'Take a look at him?'

'Yes. I had to take four stitches in his scalp, and—'

'He's gone, Doc,' interrupted Spook.

'Dead—you mean?'

'No such luck; he's vamosed.'

'Escaped, eh? Well, I guess he will have to look after his own injuries.'

And the old doctor hurried away to his horse and buggy, while Micky, Spook, and Orville sat down and the sheriff proceeded to dress himself.

'I wonder if your horse is still in the stable,' said Spook.

As soon as the sheriff was dressed, they all went to the sheriff's stable, where they found Skee Harris all tied up, gagged, and dumped into an empty manger. The horse and saddle were gone.

They untied Skee, and massaged his arms, legs, and jaw until he was able to tell them what he knew, which was not very much. He said he had played poker at the Smoke Tree Saloon until eleven o'clock, when he went to the office.

Someone there in the dark knocked him down with a blow that missed his head, but landed on the angle of his neck and shoulder. Then they gagged and bound him in the office, and a little later carried him out to the stable. He remembered their getting the cell keys from his pocket after he was in the stable.

He was able to state positively that there was more than one man, but he had no idea who they were. He said there was no conversation, as far as he heard. The muscles of his neck and shoulder were swollen and discolored, attesting to the fact that Skee had been hit very hard.

Duncan Wheeler, Frenchy Allard, and Bill Long rode into town and came over to the office, where things were explained to them.

'It don't make sense,' remarked Wheeler. 'Where did Topete steal the horse—and why did he steal it?'

Micky explained Orville's part in the incident.

'Well, now, wait a minute,' said Wheeler. 'Has anybody seen Flint Harper since yesterday? Don't you reckon Flint would have somethin' to say to Topete? I'm wonderin' if Flint didn't—'

'You think that mebbe Flint took Topete out of jail?' interrupted the sheriff.

'You don't think he'd stand for that Mexican pawin' his daughter around, do you?'

'Hell, he didn't need to knock me out,' complained Skee. 'If I'd known what he did I'd have been tempted to hang him myself.'

'I reckon I'll ride out to the Circle H,' said the sheriff.

• • •

Buck Bramer lost no time in riding out to the Circle H ranch, where Norma came out on the porch to greet him with 'Has something happened, Sheriff?'

'Well, not in the last fifteen, twenty minutes, Miss Norma,' he drawled. 'Is yore father home?'

'Why, no, he—I believe he went to Mexico with some of the boys.'

'To Mexico, eh? I wonder if he was lookin' for Topete.'

'I think he was,' nodded Norma. 'Won't you sit down?'

'Yeah, I might sit down a while, thank yuh, Norma.'

'You heard what happened out here yesterday, I suppose.'

'Well, I did hear a little. Topete got smart, eh?'

'Well, he made me very uncomfortable,' remarked Norma. 'Dad always said that Topete was a pretty decent sort of a person—but he has changed his mind.'

'What about that tenderfoot, Norma?' queried the sheriff.

'Well, he saved the situation,' smiled Norma. 'In a way it was very laughable. I was trying to get away from Topete and into the house, where I could get a weapon to defend myself; so I used the old bluff of telling him to "Look out!"

'He did it, too, but in trying to get away I tripped

and fell. Topete caught me, and just at that time Orville Woodruff appeared. He had a letter for me. I don't believe he realized the situation at all, because he walked up and held out the letter to me.

'Topete struck him in the head, knocking him flat, and the next moment Orville shot at Topete and Topete went down, striking his head on the curb of the old well. Orville was owl-eyed over what he had done, I guess. I told him I believed he had killed Topete, and he got to his feet, the queerest expression on his face.

'Then he dashed out of the patio as fast as he could run. I ran into the house, locked the door, and ran to a front window, but all I could see was a streak of dust along the road to town. It was quite a while before Topete was able to walk out of the patio, and I saw him riding away, acting like a drunken man in the saddle.'

'Yuh know,' grinned the sheriff, 'that kinda checks up. Last night Micky Davis and Spook Sullivan brought Topete to my jail and turned him over to Skee Harris, who locked him up in a cell. They charged him with stealin' a horse from Woodruff, the tenderfoot.'

'They did? Is he still in jail, Sheriff?'

'I'm mighty sorry, Norma—but he ain't. Somebody knocked Skee on the head, turned Topete loose, and left Skee all tied up in the stable. I can't imagine who turned him loose,

127

unless it was some of Topete's own gang. He's got quite a followin' in Mexico.'

'I don't believe Topete stole Orville's horse,' said Norma. 'I believe that Orville took Topete's horse, because I'm sure Topete rides a better horse and saddle than the one he took away from here yesterday.'

'Gosh, that's shore funny,' chuckled the sheriff. 'A tenderfoot shoots Topete and steals his horse. I'll bet that'll take some of the conceit out of that fancy Mexican. And,' he added thoughtfully, 'I'll betcha that if yore father catches him he'll take the rest of it out of him.'

'I suppose he will. Dad was very angry, but I hope they do not run into trouble in Mexico. Of course, if Topete was in jail they won't find him down there. Sheriff, who do you suppose stole Micky's calves?'

'Topete.'

'I wish you could convince Micky of that fact.'

'I can't—'cause I can't prove it, Norma. Oh, I know, he thinks yore father done it to break him.'

'I know he does,' sighed Norma. 'I can see Micky's angle on it; but I know that Dad wouldn't do such a thing to him.'

'Sure, he wouldn't, Norma. Yore Dad is a square shooter.'

'Sheriff,' said Norma curiously, 'did you ever see the girl that Micky goes to see in Mexico?'

'No, ma'am, I never did.'

'You know he has a girl down there, don't you?'

'No, ma'am, I don't.'

'A girl that he takes presents to down there,' persisted Norma.

'Norma,' replied the sheriff soberly, 'I'm a peace officer. My business is to be the sheriff of this here county. If it was agin the law for Micky to have a girl in Mexico, I'd sure have some information about him. As it is, I don't know a blamed thing.'

'I believe she lives in Mesquite.'

'Mexican or Injun?' queried the sheriff.

'How would I know, Sheriff?'

'Well, I'll tell yuh, Norma,' remarked the sheriff, 'if I was in yore place, I'd find out.'

'Oh, I'm not interested.'

'No-o-o, I suppose not. Why don't yuh ask Micky?'

'I did ask him—in a letter.'

'Oh, yuh did? Did he say he had a girl in Mexico?'

'Yes, he did.'

'Well, I'll betcha he has. Micky never was much of a hand to lie to folks. In Mesquite, yuh say? By golly, there's sure a lot of pretty señoritas down there. Red lips and high heels. Dance! Man, how they can dance! If I was a young feller, I'd sure look around down there.'

'Oh, you would?' snapped Norma. 'Yes, I believe men are all alike.'

'Well, I suppose they are. Yuh don't happen to know her name, do yuh?'

'I didn't feel that it was any of my business,' replied Norma.

'Well, if yuh want to know real bad—I'll ask Micky. He'd tell me, if I told him *you* wanted to know her name.'

'You needn't bother, Sheriff.'

'No bother at all, Norma.'

The sheriff got to his feet, smiling at her.

'Listen, Norma—I'm not goin' to ask Micky anythin'. I hope you find out that he ain't got a girl in Mexico; and I hope he finds out that yore father never stole his calves. Then everythin' will be lovely—I hope.'

'I am afraid you will never get your hope, Sheriff—but thanks.'

'Anyway, I'll keep on hopin', Norma. If yore father comes here before comin' to town, you can tell him that we had Topete, but he got loose. If yore father caught him, I don't want to know what happened to Topete.'

'I'll tell him—and thank you, Sheriff. Good-bye.'

'*Adios*,' grunted the sheriff, and went to his horse.

Micky, Spook, and Orville rode back home wondering who turned Topete loose. Micky was doubtful that Flint Harper did it. He was inclined to believe that Harper and Topete had been in the deal to break him.

'Yeah, and I can still see another angle,' said Spook, as they rode slowly toward the ranch. 'Suppose that mebbe Harper is all washed up with Topete. Wouldn't this be a good way to get rid of him and keep his mouth shut? Naturally he wouldn't want Skee Harris to know who lynched the Mexican.'

'Yeah, that's reasonable,' replied Micky. He lifted his head and sniffed at the breeze.

'I smell smoke,' he declared. 'Gosh, I hope that somebody hasn't started a brush fire. Everythin' is awful dry right now.'

'I can smell it, too,' declared Orville. 'Wood burning.'

The smell got stronger, and the three men spurred into a gallop for the last half mile of their journey. There was a cloud of smoke at the ranch, and as they swept in sight they saw that the stable was nearly burned down. A nearby corral fence was burning merrily.

They dismounted quickly, tied their horses at the porch, and ran down near the stable. It was too late to save any of it, but they beat out the fence fire. There had been no horses in the stable, except the palomino stallion, and they knew instinctively that the animal had been taken out. At one end of the stable was a rough shedlike structure, the oldest building on the ranch.

Apparently the direction of the wind had saved that.

Micky looked the place over grimly. There was something on the ground at the far side of the corral, and they walked over there to find the horse that Topete had ridden from the Circle H when Orville had taken the palomino. The animal, saddled and bridled, had been shot through the head.

'I just want a chance to notch a sight on Topete,' said Micky bitterly. 'He rode here, waited for us to go to town, and then shot this horse, took his own, and fired the stable.'

'I don't reckon that Flint Harper let him loose,' said Spook.

'I wouldn't be too damn sure of that,' said Micky. 'I reckon we ought to be glad he didn't set fire to the ranch house.'

'I am very much afraid that my presence in Arizona is causing you much trouble and expense, Micky,' remarked Orville sadly.

'Don't blame yourself for any of this, Red,' said Micky kindly. 'A lot of this was hatched long before you showed up. Hell, you've been a help, feller. But next time you meet Topete— shoot higher.'

'I hope I shall never have to shoot at a man again. It is not an experience that I care to repeat. Why, I scarcely knew what I was doing after I fired that shot.'

'Scarcely?' queried Spook. 'Why, you didn't know the difference between a thousand-dollar palomino stallion and a swaybacked, rat-tailed, dun-colored mare.'

'I guess I'm not of a heroic mold,' sighed Orville.

'Too damn bad you didn't kill him,' said Micky, surveying the smoldering ruins. 'Did you buy some shells for your gun?'

'They were tied to my saddle.'

'Well, I guess Topete shoots a .45. I suppose we've got to grin and bear it—until we meet Topete again.'

'Jist a moment,' said Spook, looking at Orville. 'What in the devil is a "heroic mold"?'

'Well, that is—er—a figure of speech, I suppose.'

'You git worse and worse all the time, Red,' complained Spook. 'I ask yuh what somethin' is and yuh throw the dictionary at me.'

'Well,' laughed Orville, 'you know what a hero is, I suppose.'

'Shore. He's a feller who was too damn scared to run—and got the best of it—accidently.'

'Yes, I suppose that has happened. What I meant by a heroic mold was merely a figure of speech—the mold in which a hero was made.'

'Oh, that's how they're made, eh? Figger of speech. Huh! I want to remember that. It'll go great in somebody's cow camp. So Topete got away with yore shells, eh? But yuh managed to save yore gun.'

'I gripped it in my hand all the way home, Spook.'

'That's fine. I like yore boots and yore hat. It shore gives yuh a wild, daredevil look. But never rear back in them boots. Allus keep yore balance a little ahead.'

'Thank you. But why on earth do they put such heels on boots?'

'To keep cowboys from fallin' off corral fences. It's a fact. Why, before they invented high heels for cowboy boots, the hospitals was full of broken-legged punchers who fell off fences. With them kinda heels, all yuh have to do is hook the heels over the rail, and yo're plumb safe. I figure it's one of the greatest inventions since telegrams was invented. It's shore saved more cowboys than telegrams ever did.'

'I must get me some of those spurs,' remarked Orville.

'Oh, yeah, that's right,' agreed Spook. 'Yuh never can tell when they'll need 'em.'

'When *they'll* need them?' queried Orville. 'What do you mean?'

'Oh, I see,' grinned Spook. 'You figured to use 'em for ridin' a horse. That's fine—they do use 'em for that.'

'Well, what else could they use them for, Spook?'

' 'Course, you bein' born and raised in a city, you wouldn't know how spurs happened to be invented—nor why. Well, sir, they was first invented by a one-armed undertaker in Dodge City, when they used to have a corpse for breakfast every mornin', as the sayin' goes.

'Well, them deceased was always wild cowboys, and by the time the undertaker got time to handle 'em they was usually as stiff as a board. Bein' one-handed he had a awful time handlin' 'em. But he was awful smart; so he invented spurs. 'Course, bein' good for ridin' a horse, they was sort of a double-purpose article, but he wasn't thinkin' about that when he made the first pair. His idea was to have some kinda wheels on the heels of them dead cowboys, so he could pick 'em up and jist wheel 'em to the cemetery. Smart, eh?'

'He—he really was clever,' admitted Orville. 'What is the matter, Micky?'

'I got something in my eyes,' choked Micky. He wiped away the tears and looked at Spook. 'You damn fool!' he said huskily.

'Did he throw something in your eyes, Micky?' asked Orville.

'Yeah—but you didn't see what it was,' replied Micky.

IX

Masked Bandit

Flint Harper and his men spent the night at Topete's ranch, leaving there about the middle of the morning. Topete had not come home. But Miguel Topete was no fool, decided Harper. Topete would realize that Norma would tell her father, and that Harper and his men would not hesitate about going into Mexico. Before coming back to his rancho, Topete would be very sure that none of the American cowboys were in that vicinity.

Harper and his men stopped in Encinitas, where they saw the sheriff and exchanged stories with him.

'Damn such luck!' raged Harper. 'All of us down in Mexico waiting for him—and him in jail here! But who in the devil would let him out of jail, Buck?'

'Who knows? Maybe some of his own men. You say there were five of 'em down there? Topete has a bigger following than that. In some way they knew he was in jail, I suppose. Flint, it was a good thing that Woodruff—that tenderfoot—was out there.'

Flint Harper nodded grimly. 'That's true, Buck.

Well, I guess we better be goin'. The boys are pretty tired and hungry. We noticed smoke over toward Davis's place as we came back. I hope it ain't a brush fire gettin' loose in the hills.'

'I guess I better ride out that way,' replied the sheriff.

The boys at the Bar D had finished their meal when the sheriff rode in alone. The burned stable explained the smoke. Micky showed him the dead horse, and the sheriff swore quietly.

'That's his revenge,' said the sheriff. 'Half Yaqui, half Mexican, all savage. Waited until you fellers went to town. He's bad. If you see him—shoot quick.'

'I hope to tell you,' nodded Micky grimly. 'And if I don't see him pretty soon—I'm ridin' into Mexico.'

'He told Norma Harper that he was sellin' out his cattle. He'll prob'ly turn bandit and start raidin'. Keep your eyes peeled, boys.'

'I want his ears for my collection,' said Spook soberly.

After the sheriff rode away, Orville said to Spook:

'I—I believe I have read of—er—ear collectors. Savages, I believe. You don't collect them, do you, Spook?'

'Well, I've only got two, so far.'

'Whose?'

'Mine.'

'Just for that, Orville, you've got to wash the dishes,' said Micky. 'And the ear collector can wipe 'em.'

'What are you goin' to do?' asked the aggrieved Spook, who hated to wash or wipe dishes.

'I'm goin' to sit down and do some hard thinkin'.'

'Any thinkin' you do will be awful hard, Micky. You ought to watch him think, Red. It's downright sufferin'. Face all twisted out of shape, eyes buggin' out, hands clenched. Why, I asked him one day if he knowed what month Christmas came in, and before he got through tryin' to figure it out he was a physical and mental wreck for three days. It shore takes a lot out of him.'

'Is that so?' queried Orville innocently.

'I should say it is. Never ask him a question. Oh, you can ask him how he feels, or anythin' like that, without him goin' into a decline. You know, one time I said, "Micky, which way is the north star from here?" Do you know what he done? Why, he laid out there on a hill for three nights workin' with a compass. Fact!'

'Did he find out which way it was?' asked Orville.

'How in hell could he?'

'Well, why couldn't he?'

'He didn't know which one was the north star.'

'Red!' called Micky from the main room. 'Do you know who is the biggest damn liar in Arizona?'

'Sh-h-h,' warned Spook. 'Don't git him started on that.'

'Is there a *biggest* liar in this State?' queried Orville.

'Now you *have* ruined him,' wailed Spook. 'There's more liars in the State of Arizony than there is stars in the sky—and look what the north star done to him.'

'I'm sorry,' said Orville.

'I should hope you would be,' said Spook, splashing water in the dishpan.

'Don't you use soap in washing dishes, Spook?'

'Soap? In washin' dishes? Not me. I don't want any soap taste in my food. Anyway, this ain't dirt—it's food.'

'I *always* use soap,' called Micky.

'All right, you damn dudes; it's two to one. You ain't gettin' very far with your thinkin', are you, Micky?'

'Goin' good, thank you.'

'What are you thinkin' right now?'

'If you knew, your ears would set your hair on fire.'

'See what I told you?' gloated Spook. 'When he's in that kinda shape he can't give an intelligent answer.'

'I think he is rather intelligent,' said Orville, grinning.

'You do, huh? Then you better go in there and set beside him. Two souls without a single thought.'

'No,' laughed Orville, 'I would rather sit in the shade of the porch and look at the country. The immensity of it rather awes me, Spook.'

Spook dropped a frying pan on the floor and looked wide-eyed at Orville.

'It does what to yuh?' he gasped.

'Awes me.'

'Oh, yeah. Awe, eh? Well, I can stand for it if the country can. But words like that indicates a wasted youth. They call it eddication. Mebbe it is, but what good is it? You look at this country and says it awes yuh. I look at it and I say, "Yo're a hell of a lookin' pile of dry brush, busted earth, and hot days." '

'But it is so immense, Spook.'

'So's the moon, Red. But yuh don't hear me ravin' about its size. Well, there's them damn dishes all done again. The only advantage I ever seen in washin' dishes was that it gits yore hands clean. Let's go set on the porch. No, don't go in there while Micky's thinkin'. He's as dangerous as a lobo wolf.'

'Does he ever arrive at a conclusion, Spook?'

'Hu-u-uh?'

'I mean, does his thinking ever amount to anything?'

'Well, it never has—as far as I've seen.'

They sat down on the porch steps, looking at the remains of their stable. Orville said quietly:

'I wonder why Topete did not revenge himself upon me, instead of burning Micky's stable and killing his horse.'

'Don't worry, Red—he will.'

'You mean—he will still seek revenge for what I did to him?'

'Why, I hope to tell yuh.'

'Well! That doesn't make me feel so secure, Spook.'

'Aw, I wouldn't worry about it, Red. Topete will shoot yuh from behind. He allus does. He's a pretty good shot, too.'

'What satisfaction is that, Spook?'

'Well, yuh won't never know what hit yuh. One minute you'll be in the full bloom of youth—and the next minute'—Spook lowered his voice huskily—'you'll be jist a withered leaf from the tree of life.'

Orville winced visibly. 'If he would only consider the fact that I—I did it all in self-defense, Spook.'

'But he won't—that's the whole trouble. Self-defense don't mean a thing to Topete. He's jist plumb savage. 'Course it all depends on how he's feelin' the day he decides to kill yuh. Mebbe he'll knock yuh off quick. Why, I've knowed him to rope a victim and drag him all the way down across the border.'

'The—the man died?'

'Yeah, he shore did. Starved to death.'

'Starved to death?'

'That's right. His neck was stretched so long that he never could git food all the way down to his stummick.'

'That,' declared Orville, 'doesn't sound like the truth, Spook.'

'I didn't believe it myself, Red. But that's the trouble with a country that gits yuh all awed-up thataway; there's queer things happenin'. How are yuh comin', Micky?'

'Well,' replied Micky from inside the house, 'if I handled the truth as careless as you do, I'd say everythin' was all right.'

'Aw, jist let it go,' said Spook. 'Soon as I git a couple minutes to spare, I'll work out yore problem. No use you gettin' yore brain all het up. Let a deep thinker do the job.'

'Are you a deep thinker, Spook?' queried Orville.

'So damn deep that his thoughts never get to the surface,' said Micky.

At times the gambling play at the Smoke Tree Saloon and Gambling House, in Encinitas, was fairly heavy, but tonight there was only a draw-poker table working. Flint Harper, Duncan Wheeler, Buck Bramer, Skee Harris, Doctor Mitchell, and Ed Ross, the proprietor, were playing.

It was nearly midnight when Skee Harris said:

'There ought to be somethin' done about Topete.'

'There will be—if I ever catch him across the border,' stated Flint Harper grimly, as he shuffled the cards.

'I wonder if he *did* get Micky Davis's yearlin's.'

'I'm not a damn bit interested in Micky Davis's yearlin's,' said Harper.

'Can you imagine that damned Mexican goin' out there, shootin' that old mare, and then firin' the stable, after he got his own horse?' said Skee. 'I can't figure a jasper like that.'

'He won't dare come across the border again,' said Buck Bramer.

Doctor Mitchell yawned and looked at his watch.

'It is time for me to go to bed,' he announced. 'Anyway, I have donated plenty to all of you; so I shall tell you all good night, gentlemen.'

'Might as well make it unanimous,' said Flint Harper, shoving back his chair.

Ed Ross cashed all the chips and put them in the rack, preparatory to taking them back to his little private office.

'There's a drink comin'—on the house,' he announced, as he got to his feet and started back to his little office.

The other men stepped over to the bar to get their nightcap.

'There's somethin' funny about this whole deal,'

remarked the sheriff. 'Ain't nobody explained how that tenderfoot disappeared from the stage between here and Pancho's Place, and how he got to Davis's ranch. Davis introduces him as his cousin, which he prob'ly ain't.'

'Micky Davis acts like he's close-herdin' the feller,' said Wheeler, pouring himself a drink. 'And who in hell stole that skeleton?'

'Well,' said Skee Harris, 'I'll bet big odds that Spook Sullivan didn't.'

'I'd like to know who took Topete out of my jail,' growled the sheriff. 'I suppose I can charge that up to his own—'

Every man jerked back from the bar, looking around quickly. From somewhere came the unmistakable report of a gun. Skee Harris ran toward the doorway, but the rest of the men were undecided.

'Sounded to me like it was out the other way,' said the sheriff.

They were all listening closely. Skee Harris, stopped at the doorway, was leaning out, looking up and down the street.

'Nobody out this way,' he told them.

'I just wonder—' began the sheriff, and ran back to the door of Ed Ross's office, the other men following him.

He jerked the door open, and a breeze from an open window blew powder smoke into the saloon. Ed Ross was on his back, a gun on the floor near his right hand, the little safe door wide open.

Doctor Mitchell shoved the sheriff aside and knelt down beside Ross. The owner of the Smoke Tree was not dead. The bullet had creased the side of his head, tearing the scalp badly, but it was not dangerous, barring a possible concussion.

Ross opened his eyes as the doctor examined the torn scalp. Ross winced from the pain.

'You're all right, Ed,' assured the doctor. 'Who was it?'

'Topete,' whispered the injured saloon man. 'Made me empty the safe. I—I took a chance and went for my gun.'

'How much did he get, Ed?' asked the sheriff.

'About eleven hundred dollars,' whispered Ross.

'The nerve of that damn bandit!' snapped the sheriff.

'Masked,' whispered Ross. 'The poor fool.'

Ross promptly fainted after giving them the information, and they carried him down to the doctor's home.

'Skee,' said the sheriff, as they went back to the office, 'there won't be anybody safe around here until we get that feller. Right now he's a *mucho malo hombre*—and he ain't through yet.'

'What do yuh reckon I ort to do—start runnin'?' queried Skee peevishly. 'You don't need to tell me that he's a bad boy—and he's got some bad friends.'

'He's jist a ignorant bandit, Skee.'

'Yeah—and his bullets are jist as hot as though he had all the brains in the world. I tell yuh, Topete was awful dumb when they brought him to me. He'd been hit on the head pretty solid. He'd say, *"No comprender"* when me and Doc asked him questions.'

'I wonder what went wrong with him. Usually he's plumb full of talk. I wish you'd have kept him in jail, Skee. It would have saved the Smoke Tree eleven hundred dollars, and a knock on the head for Ross.'

'And a knock on the head for *me,*' added Skee. 'But I don't guess that amounts to much. I'm jist the jailer around here. You act like I *turned* him loose. Mebbe you think I pounded my own head with a gun barrel and then tied myself up in the stable.'

'No, Skee, I don't figure it that way. You was a victim of circumstances.'

'I was a victim of Mexicans, I tell yuh. Topete's own gang must have jumped me.'

'I reckon so. If we only had him in jail—I mean, if he hadn't got out—'

'Yeah! But he's out, so what's the use talkin' about it?'

'I reckon we better go to bed, Skee. First thing I know you'll be peevish. Yo're gettin' so that a feller can't talk with yuh. I'm not chidin' yuh for lettin' Topete get away. Might happen to anybody, if they was half-asleep from playin' poker in a poor light.'

'All right, Buck, we'll go to bed,' sighed Skee. 'You win.'

Buck Bramer, the sheriff, spent some time next morning posting notices around the town, offering two thousand dollars reward for Miguel Topete, dead or alive. Micky Davis, Spook Sullivan, and Orville Woodruff came to town on their way out to Lobo Solo Canyon and learned of the holdup and attempted murder at the Smoke Tree Saloon.

'And the next thing you know,' said Spook as they rode on, 'Miguel Topete is goin' to make some raids. He'll take his gang on this side of the border and raise hell. They're prob'ly rustlin' cattle right now.'

'More likely rustlin' horses,' said Micky. 'They're easy to dispose of down there.'

'Why isn't it taken up with the Mexican Government?' asked Orville.

'Too much red tape,' replied Micky. 'By the time they'd be convinced that somethin' should be done about Topete, he'd die of old age. There's only one procedure—shoot the son of a buck.'

'But isn't it illegal to make an armed invasion into Mexico?'

'Shore it is. But who can prove that we did—or will? It ain't legal for any of us to pack a six-gun into Mexico, but I'd hate to be caught down there without a gun—law or no law.'

'If we should happen to meet Topete,' propounded Orville, 'would we attempt to capture him?'

There are times, Red,' said Spook, 'when I jest have to stare at you and say *tck, tck, tck.* I like you fine, feller, but your intelligence amazes me more every day. If we should happen to meet Mr. Topete, you yank out that old hawg-leg you're packin', point it in his general direction, and unhook all the hell that's inside it.'

'And don't shoot at his feet,' added Micky.

It was a long ride out to Pancho's Place. From there they went east, across the brushy, broken hills, to the rim of Lobo Solo Canyon. For miles this canyon was hundreds of feet deep, with sheer, rocky walls. If there were any trails into this part of the canyon, Micky and Spook had never heard about one.

At a point almost due east of Encinitas, there was a sheer drop of possibly seventy-five feet in the canyon bed, indicating that there had been an ancient waterfall there at some time. Below this were a number of trails leading down into the canyon, but the old waterfall blocked anyone's entering the upper part of the canyon.

They rested on the rim of the canyon in the shade of a juniper, and watched the buzzards planing far out over the depths. Eagles soared in close to the cliffs, and quail called from the brush along the canyon rim.

'Does that look like the canyon you was in, Red?' asked Spook.

'Well, I suppose there is a resemblance,' replied Orville. 'My view of the place was at night and from the bottom, you know.'

'I reckon there is a bottom,' remarked Micky, 'but I've never seen much of it. I dunno,' he said reflectively. 'Red says he was in a deep canyon, and I can't quite figure on anybody stealin' him at Pancho's Place and goin' miles and miles to take him into the canyon. 'Course, we haven't any way to time it. The stage gets into Pancho's Place at a certain time. We could check on that. But Red don't know what time he got into the canyon, so timin' the stage won't do any good.'

'Looking back at the incident,' said Orville, 'I don't suppose it took us over an hour to make the journey.'

'Could you be sure of that?' asked Micky eagerly.

'Not exactly, of course. At that time I had never been on a horse before. Naturally, I was worried over my predicament, and I was not entirely recovered from my indiscretions in Sierra Vista. Still, I feel reasonably certain that it did not take over an hour to make the journey that night.'

'Talks like a damn dictionary,' sighed Spook. 'Now, if I'd been in his place, and you'd asked me that same question, I'd have cut out all the frills and said, "Hell, yeah!" '

'I wish I had wings,' said Micky, gazing into the depths. 'I'd like to drop down into that canyon.'

'You can twist that around,' grinned Spook. 'Just drop down into that canyon and you'll shore get you a couple wings.'

Micky twisted his head and looked at the sun.

'We better be movin',' he said. 'It'll take quite a while to ride this rim, and I don't like to hunt for trails in the dark.'

They mounted their horses and went slowly down through the brush. Small side canyons caused them to make wide detours, and in places the brush was so thick along the rim that they were obliged to circle wide. About three miles south of where they had rested they ran into a small bunch of cattle. There were at least twenty yearlings in the bunch of grown steers, but close inspection showed that they belonged to the Box JB. There were a number of Circle H steers in the bunch.

They were looking over the herd when a shot echoed back from the cliffs, rattling back and forth until it died away. The three riders were grouped together, wondering about the shot.

Spook said:

'Prob'ly somebody gettin' a piece of venison, Micky.'

'Mebbe,' said Micky. 'Stay here.'

Micky whirled his horse and rode swiftly to the left, heading for a rocky pinnacle where he could get a view of the country below them. At the foot of the pinnacle, he dismounted and climbed up on the rocks, where he stood for possibly five minutes. Then he sprang down, mounted his horse, and spurred down to them.

'Topete!' he exclaimed. 'He's a mile or more down the rim by this time, goin' like hell on that palomino. I seen him plain.'

'What the hell's he been up to now?' grunted Spook. 'Or mebbe somebody took a shot at him, Micky.'

'Can't we catch him?' asked Orville.

Micky shook his head. 'Not with a lead like that, Red. That palomino is awful fast. We wouldn't have a chance on earth.'

'I would like to own that horse,' said Orville.

'Who wouldn't?' queried Spook. 'You had him once, Red.'

'And didn't know it,' sighed Orville.

They rode on down the rim, but did not see anyone. It was nearly dark when they turned from the canyon and rode past the Circle H, going directly to Encinitas, and from there back to the Bar D. Orville was a very weary young man, but did not complain.

'I believe he's got what it takes to make a cowpuncher,' said Micky admiringly.

'Yeah—lack of brains,' agreed Spook wearily.

151

● ● ●

It was late afternoon when Flint Harper and one of his men galloped into Encinitas. They stopped at Doctor Mitchell's house, and then went straight to the sheriff's office.

'More hell, Buck,' said Harper grimly. 'Somebody shot Ted Byers yesterday—out near Lobo Solo Canyon.'

Ted Byers was one of the Harper cowboys.

'Kill him?' the sheriff asked.

'He isn't dead yet. I'm sendin' Mitchell out to work on him. Ted and Joe Nevins were pickin' up a bunch of young stuff out there, and got separated late in the afternoon. Joe heard the shot fired and thought maybe Ted shot at a rattler or a coyote. He tried to find Ted, but couldn't, although he stayed out there until after dark. Ted didn't come home last night, so we all went searchin' for him early this mornin'. We found him out there, shot up pretty bad—a rifle bullet through his right shoulder.'

'Can you imagine that?' snorted the sheriff. 'Who the devil would shoot that kid?'

'I'm not accusin' anybody,' replied Harper coldly, 'but Joe saw Davis, Sullivan, and that tenderfoot out there along the canyon after the shot was fired. They wasn't close enough for Joe to attract their attention; he recognized 'em.'

'That don't sound so awful good,' mused the

152

sheriff. 'Still, it don't make sense. They ain't got anything against Ted Byers.'

'They're against me,' reminded Harper.

'Yeah, that's true. I hope Ted recovers and is able to tell who shot him—if he knows. In the meantime, I'll drift out to the Bar D and kinda have a talk with the boys. Somethin' might come of it, you know.'

X

A Note

Hard work never did appeal to Spook Sullivan. He sat on the porch of the ranch house, shoulders hunched against the wall, a picture of perfect contentment. On his lap was the old rusty revolver which they had found with the skeleton. Beside Spook was a saucer of kerosene and several old rags, together with a broken file, a screwdriver, and a few nails.

Orville Woodruff sat in a broken-backed rocker, his stockinged feet on the porch rail, while Micky sat on the steps reading an old magazine.

' 'Course you're sore, Red,' said Spook. 'Ridin' all that distance naturally makes you sore. But'—Spook squinted at the old gun—'think how the horse must feel. You was jest a passenger.'

'Yes, I suppose that's true,' sighed Orville. 'I wish we knew why Topete fired that shot—if he fired it.'

'Either Topete fired it or somebody fired at Topete,' said Micky, looking up from his magazine. 'He was shore travelin' fast when I seen him.'

'He's goin' to fool around on this side of the

border until somebody rubs him out with a hot bullet,' said Spook, digging at the hard dirt in the muzzle of the old gun. 'Man, this dirt is almost petrified. Jest like diggin' into rock.'

'Prob'ly all rusted,' said Micky.

'Not so bad. It was protected from the weather in that crevice. Them old shells would be corroded all to nothin' if the rain ever got to it. 'Course they're in bad shape.'

'It isn't worth the bother,' said Orville.

'No bother,' said Spook, grinning. 'I like to do this kinda stuff. It's fun to monkey with old guns this a way.'

'Put it away, Spook,' said Micky quietly. 'Here comes Buck Bramer.'

Spook took the gun and his tools into the house before the sheriff rode up, then came back to the porch. After an exchange of greetings, the sheriff came and sat on the porch.

'Any trace of yore yearlin's, Micky?' asked the sheriff.

'Not a trace, Buck. The three of us prospected the rim of Lobo Solo yesterday from the top to this side of the old falls, but we didn't find any of my missin' yearlin's.'

'Mebbe you were right when you said that Topete took them over the border.'

Micky nodded thoughtfully. 'Speakin' of Topete—I seen him yesterday.'

'You seen him? Where?'

155

'Out there along Lobo Solo. We was huntin' calves, and we heard a shot. I rode up on a pinnacle, where I got a fair view. You know how broken and brushy it is out there. After a while I seen Topete on his palomino, goin' like hell, far down along the canyon. I don't know whether he fired the shot or somebody shot at him. We didn't see him again.'

'You heard the shot, huh?'

Micky looked quickly at the sheriff.

'Why—yeah, we heard it. Did anybody else hear it?'

'Joe Nevin heard it, too.'

'He did, eh? Well,' said Micky, 'it made plenty noise.'

'And the bullet hit Ted Byers.'

'No! The devil it did! Did it kill him?'

The sheriff explained what Flint Harper had told him, and about Joe Nevin's seeing them at long distance.

'I see,' nodded Micky quietly. 'And Flint Harper thought we shot Ted. Yeah, *he* would.'

The sheriff rubbed his chin thoughtfully. 'Well, you can't blame Flint for his suspicions, Micky. But why would Topete shoot him?'

'Mebbe,' suggested Spook, 'he's declared war on the United States.'

'Well, it looks to me as though we've got to stop Mr. Topete,' said the sheriff. 'We're offerin' two thousand, dead or alive. I'm not in any position to invade Mexico, so I'll have to wait and get him on this side of the line.'

'Buck,' said Micky, 'you know how I feel toward Flint Harper. I don't believe it's any secret in Smoke Tree Valley. But you can tell him for me that if he wants to go into Mexico after that murderin' skunk, me and Spook will go along. I've got a settlement to make with that hombre myself.'

'I'll tell him, Micky.'

'And as far as I'm personally concerned, Flint can believe that Topete fired that shot—or not. If Ted recovers he can shore tell 'em that none of us shot him.'

'I'll tell him,' promised the sheriff. 'Your story sets right with me—and Flint is no fool.'

'I'll admit that—after figurin' out his scheme to break me.'

The sheriff rode away, satisfied in his own mind that Micky was telling the truth. Spook recovered his gun and tools and went to work on the gun again. Micky was mad.

'Tryin' to put the deadwood on us for shootin' Ted Byers. Why, Ted is only a kid. He'd be the *last* one of that gang I'd shoot. When I break loose, it'll be against Flint Harper—not his hired hands.'

'Love o' Mike!' gasped Spook. 'Look! A hunk of paper in the gun barrel, Micky!'

Micky and Orville joined Spook quickly. He had a discolored piece of paper, folded tightly, which he had dug out of the barrel of the old gun. Micky took it and unfolded it carefully. It was the front half of an envelope, the postmark and address faded to nothing. But on the back were penciled words, clearly decipherable. It read:

Shot twice and left arm broke. Can't get away. Notify my wife at 1236 Ross Street, San Francisco. My gold mine is under my shack and I want her to get this.

JACK WOODRUFF

Micky read it aloud, then handed the note to Orville.

'Can you imagine that?' queried Spook. 'He left the note in his gun barrel, figurin', mebbe, that the sheriff would find it.'

'And then lived to carve his name on the rock,' added Micky. 'If he had only written the names of the men who shot him!'

'I guess he did his best,' said Orville. 'I wish I had known him.'

'But you're just about as well off as you was before,' said Spook. 'Where in the devil do you suppose his shack was located fifteen years ago? There's old shacks scattered all over these hills, where prospectors worked in the minin' days.'

'I doubt that it will ever be found,' said Orville. 'Those directions are too vague.'

'I'm not so darned sure of that,' remarked Micky. 'There must be somebody in this valley who knew where he lived.'

'We could do a lot of askin',' said Spook.

'Don't do any askin',' replied Micky quickly.

'Do you think there's still somebody—'

'What do you suppose they kidnapped Orville for? Have a little sense. Don't mention that note. Wherever that mine is, it's so rich that men will murder to get their hands on it.'

'Sweet daisies!' gasped Spook. 'I'm almost scared that we found it. Can I ask you a question, Micky?'

'Go ahead!'

'When do we eat? I'm hongry.'

'Go peel some spuds, if you're so hongry.'

'That's jest my luck! Every time I open my mouth I put my foot in it. Make the discovery of the century—and have to peel spuds.'

It was after dark that evening when six riders stopped at the Bar D ranch house. Flint Harper, Duncan Wheeler, and Skee Harris, grim of face, came into the main room, where Micky Davis, Spook Sullivan, and Orville Woodruff looked them over curiously.

'Ted Byers died this evenin',' stated Flint Harper. 'He was conscious long enough to tell us that Topete shot him. He was too far gone to

159

give us any details. We're goin' down to find Topete.'

'That's fine,' nodded Micky. 'Me and Spook are with you.'

'What about me?' asked Orville.

'You're stayin' right here,' replied Micky firmly. 'This is not your battle, young man.'

'He knocked me down,' reminded Orville.

'I want to thank you for what you done out there, Woodruff,' said Flint Harper. 'It was lucky that you showed up.'

'You are welcome, I'm sure,' answered Orville. 'It was the greatest scare of my life.'

'We'll saddle up right away,' said Micky.

'Don't hurry,' said Wheeler. 'We've got to wait for Frenchy Allard.'

'Where's he?' asked Spook.

'Bill Long is sick,' replied Wheeler. 'Bilious attack, I reckon. Me and Frenchy came to town to get some medicine for him. When this deal came up I sent Frenchy back with the medicine. He'll go to Encinitas, and they'll send him out here.'

Micky and Spook were leading their horses up to the porch when Frenchy Allard galloped up from Encinitas. He said that Bill was not any better, but wanted to come along.

'Bill would like to get a crack at Topete,' said Frenchy.

'Who wouldn't?' retorted Spook.

They rode away, leaving Orville on the porch, watching them drift out in the darkness.

Ted Byers's body had been taken to Encinitas by Doctor Mitchell. Norma was not afraid to stay there with only Sing Low. She promised to lock the ranch house and not go outside that evening.

It was just growing dark when Sing Low came to and called to her in the main room:

'Missy! Ol' woman wan' speek with you.'

'An old woman?' queried Norma.

'Yessa. Ol' woman on mule.'

'That's a queer description, Sing. Where is she?'

'By klitchen do'.'

It was old Grandma Ramirez, astride an old burro, which was led by a young peon, barefooted, but with a dirty serape around his thin shoulders. Norma had never seen the old lady before.

'*Si, señorita*,' replied the old lady. 'Theese ees not Meeky's rancho?'

'Micky's rancho? Do you mean Micky Davis?'

'*Si, si*!'

'Why, no. This is Harper's ranch. Did you come from Mexico?'

'*Si*, from *Mejico*.'

'Why, you came too far. Micky's rancho is half-way back to the border.'

'*Por Dios*!' she muttered softly. '*Gracias, señorita*. But how can I find?'

There was something pathetic about the little

old lady, the tired burro, and the sore-footed peon.

'You are weary and hungry,' said Norma. 'Come in and we will give you food.'

'*Gracias*,' said the old lady. 'We are tired and 'ungry, but we mus' find Meeky.'

'Why do you have to find Micky?' asked Norma, her curiosity mounting.

'Meeky is my leetle *amigo*,' she said slowly. 'I mus' see heem.'

'Your little friend?' said Norma. 'Come. You have plenty of time. Some food will make you strong for the return.'

Slowly, the old lady slid off the back of the burro, which sighed with relief. The young peon dropped the rope and followed the little old lady into the house. Grandma Ramirez wore a gay calico waist, a badly fitting, rusty black skirt, and high-heeled shoes. Around her head was a bright-colored handkerchief. She sat down in a chair, while the peon squatted against the walls, his brown eyes bright in the lamplight, as he surveyed the furnishing of the room.

Norma ordered Sing Low to prepare a meal. The little Chinaman looked with disapproval upon the guests, but obeyed orders by banging pans in the kitchen at a great rate.

'You say that Micky is your friend?' queried Norma.

'*Si, señorita.*'

'Your name?'

'I am Juana Ramirez, *señorita*. Meeky call me *dulce amiga*.'

She said it very proudly, but with a twinkle in her old eyes.

'He calls you sweetheart?' smiled Norma. 'But he has another sweetheart in Mexico.'

'No, *señorita*. Meeky's sweetheart ees Americano.'

'I have heard that he has a sweetheart in Mexico to whom he takes many presents.'

'Of this I do not know—but I do not believe. Meeky breeng me many presents. This waist, this shoes—everytheeng he breeng to me.'

'But he must have a sweetheart in Mexico,' insisted Norma. 'In Mesquite, perhaps.'

Grandma Ramirez turned and fired a volley of Mexican at the young peon, who shook his head as he replied to her question. She turned to Norma.

'Chico say Meeky not come to Mesquite to see girl.'

'Why do you wish to see Micky?' asked Norma.

'Sometheeng I weesh to tell Meeky—alone, *señorita*. It ees ver' *importante*.'

While Grandma Ramirez and Chico ate supper, Norma wondered what was important enough to bring this very old lady all the way over the border to see Micky Davis. She also wondered if this was the 'woman in Mexico' who was the recipient of Micky's presents. However, Norma had made up her mind what to do.

'If this is important,' she told the old lady, 'I'll hitch up the buckboard team and take you to Micky. It will take too long for you to go there on the burro, and you might get lost. Chico can stay here while we are gone.'

'*Gracias, señorita*; you are ver' kind—and it ees *importante*.'

For an hour or more after the posse had left the ranch, Orville wandered nervously about. He tried to read, but could not keep his mind on the printed page. He cleaned and oiled the gun that Spook had loaned him, and placed it on the stone mantel of the fireplace. Every sound outside, every creak of the ranch house, annoyed him. He drew the curtains aside and peered out into the night. A coyote chorus gave him goose pimples.

Finally he decided to ignore everything, sat down in an old rocker beside the table. He tried to get interested in a magazine story, but found himself skipping the description and reading only the dialogue. He relaxed and shut his eyes. It was then that he heard the soft creak of the kitchen door, the very faint scruff of a boot-sole on the wooden floor. Someone was in the kitchen. There was an open doorway between the kitchen and the main room.

Slowly, he laid the magazine aside. The gun on the mantel seemed miles away, but it was his only defense. With his knees knocking together he got to his feet, feigned a yawn, and started slowly toward the mantel.

'*Alto!*' said a voice sharply, and Orville nearly collapsed.

'Oh!' he grunted and stopped. Slowly he turned. Just inside the doorway stood Topete! He wore a black mask, covering his head. Lamplight glittered on his silver ornaments. A big black revolver in his huge right hand was covering Orville. Topete laughed harshly.

'So they hunt Topete, huh?' he growled.

'Ye-yes,' faltered Orville. 'I—I believe that is their plans.'

'They theenk I am in Mexico, huh? Fools! Face the wall! So! Hands behind. You are not a fool, *señor.*'

'I—I doubt that,' faltered Orville, gazing longingly at the gun on the mantel.

Orville's hands were quickly tied, then Topete proceeded to gag him with a wad of cloth and a long strip of the same material. Then he shoved Orville into a chair and roped him tightly to it.

He searched Orville's pockets thoroughly, then proceeded to make a search of the entire ranch house. Orville could hear him in the different parts of the house, throwing things about in his search. This search possibly required thirty minutes. Then he came back and sat down, while he deftly rolled a cigarette.

Judging from his attitude and lack of haste, he was undecided what to do next. He finished the cigarette, snapped the butt into the fireplace, and leaned back, studying Orville through the eye slits in his mask.

Suddenly he jerked to attention. From outside came the rattle of iron-shod wheels on gravel, the thud of trotting hoofs. Topete was on his feet, gun drawn. With the stride of a hunting cat he reached a front window and carefully drew the shade aside. Then he stepped against the wall and near the door.

There were footsteps on the porch, and Norma's voice called:

'Micky! Oh, Micky!'

'Come,' called Topete quietly, and Norma opened the door.

She was inside the room before she saw Topete; then it was too late to draw back. Topete was only a foot away from her, laughing behind his mask.

'So we meet again, *señorita*,' he said huskily. 'That ees good!'

As he reached for her, she struck him in the face, the blow landing solidly, but he only laughed. She struck again, tearing away his mask. Spitting out a curse, he struck her on the chin with his right hand, knocking her through the doorway, where she collapsed in a pitiful heap.

XI

A Kidnaping

It was past midnight when the nine riders surrounded the huddle of adobe shacks which were the ranch houses of Miguel Topete. There were no lights. A swift search of the corral and tumbledown stable showed that there were no horses or riding equipment, indicating that no riders were at the rancho.

They broke into the ranch house and made a complete search, which netted them exactly nothing. Disgruntled over their failure to find Topete, they grouped together to discuss further plans. It was about eight miles from there to Mesquite, and some wanted to go there.

'That might cause complications,' said Harper. 'If we found him there and started anythin', we'd prob'ly have to buck soldiers. No; I believe we should stay here until he returns.'

'That's how I feel about it, too,' added Duncan Wheeler.

'If you want my opinion,' said Micky, 'I'd say that Topete's on the other side of the border, holed up with some friend.'

'I don't think your opinion is worth a dime,' said Harper.

'All right,' said Micky coldly. 'If you want to stay here—that is your privilege. Personally, I believe that Topete is too smart to come down here. You came here once, Harper, and he'd feel that you'd come again. While we're all down there chasin' wild geese, we're givin' him a sweet chance to pull somethin' more. I'm goin' back right now.'

'Afraid he'll run away with your tenderfoot?' asked Allard.

'That tenderfoot can take care of himself,' replied Micky. 'C'mon, Spook.'

'Davis may be right,' said Harper. 'We'll all go back.'

Micky and Spook led the way back to an old road that led into the road to the Bar D; then they left the others and went on home. The oil lamp in the main room was almost dry, the chimney badly smoked. Orville was gone. They searched the place and came back to the main room.

'Where in the devil has he gone, do you suppose?' said Micky anxiously. 'There's his gun on the fireplace, and his hat's hangin' on a chair.'

Spook lighted a lantern, and they went down to the corral, where they found Orville's horse. He had not gone away on horseback. They came back to the porch, where Micky saw buggy tracks. By the aid of the lantern light they examined the tracks. Apparently the buggy or buckboard had stopped close to the porch, and in going away it had turned very abruptly.

'Somebody must have come here since we left,' said Spook. 'I know danged well those tracks wasn't there before dark. Whoever it was, they took Red with 'em.'

'And without his hat or gun,' said Micky. 'I don't like it, Spook.'

'Yeah, it shore looks as though he went in a hurry.'

Micky stepped up on the porch, where the rays of the lantern illuminated the wooden floor. There was a spatter of drops—dark-colored. Micky got down and looked closely.

'I believe it's blood,' he said quietly. 'I don't know what else it could be, Spook.'

'What's our next move, Micky?'

'When you can't think of anythin' to do—do somethin',' replied Micky. 'Let's go to Encinitas, followin' those buggy tracks. They didn't go south, over that old road, or we'd have noticed 'em. They must have gone north. Let's go.'

It was too dark to watch for tracks along the road. They found that only Duncan Wheeler, Frenchy Allard, and Skee Harris stopped at Encinitas. They were at the bar in the Smoke Tree Saloon, talking with Buck Bramer, the sheriff, when Micky and Spook came in.

'Did Norma Harper come to your ranch in a buckboard tonight, Micky?' asked the sheriff.

'There wasn't *anybody* at the ranch,' replied Micky. 'That's why we came on. What about Norma Harper?'

'I didn't get a chance to ask Flint Harper about it when they went through. About eight o'clock Norma drove through here in a buckboard. I was crossin' the street just ahead of her, and she spoke to me. It looked like a woman with her, but I can't be sure. Your ranch is the only place south of here. The boys say that they came in over the old road, but there wasn't any wheel tracks.'

'Didn't you see her go back, Buck?' asked Micky anxiously.

'She didn't go back through here, 'cause I kept watch. After she was gone, I kinda wondered about her, but expected she'd be back.'

'Wasn't Woodruff at your ranch?' asked Skee Harris.

'No,' replied Micky. 'There wasn't anybody at my ranch—and there was fresh wheel tracks at the porch.'

'I wish I'd stopped her,' sighed the sheriff. 'I always think of the right thing to do—afterwards.'

'Oh, she must have gone back,' insisted Spook. 'You missed seein' her, Buck.'

'I did not, I tell you. I watched that street like a hawk.'

'Mebbe she went around the town.'

'If you could tell me *why* she would, I might admit that she could have done that.'

'And another woman was ridin' with her,' mused Micky. 'What woman?'

'Might have been a man lookin' like a woman,' said Allard.

'It could,' agreed the sheriff. 'The light wasn't very good. But it was Norma Harper drivin' that sorrel team.'

'I reckon we better wait here,' said Micky. 'If there's anythin' wrong, Harper will be back.'

They sat down around a card table and talked. Ross was getting along all right. They talked about the killing of Ted Byers.

'There's no use plannin' on how to get Topete,' said Duncan Wheeler. 'Sooner or later, he'll make a fool break.'

'I've offered two thousand dollars for him,' said the sheriff. 'As soon as I can take the matter up again, I believe we can offer a bigger reward. Ed Ross has boosted it five hundred dollars.'

'Get a reward big enough,' said Wheeler, 'and somebody is goin' to collect it.'

'That's what I figure, Dunc. I shore hope that Topete ain't had nothin' to do with this deal tonight.'

They had sat and talked for more than an hour when they heard the thud of hoofs coming down the street. Flint Harper and his four men drew up in front of the saloon. Behind Flint rode a wide-eyed kid—Chico, the peon who had brought Grandma Ramirez to the Circle H.

They all came quickly into the saloon. Flint Harper singled out Micky and came to him.

'Davis, I want to—'

'Wait a minute,' interrupted Micky. 'Me and Spook went to the ranch. There wasn't anybody there. We found buggy tracks near the porch— tracks that wasn't there when we rode away.'

'Woodruff gone?' asked Harper weakly.

'Not a soul at the place. That's why we came here. Listen to what Buck has to tell. He seen Norma go through here—'

'I know about that. This Mexican kid told us. He can't talk much English, but Joe Nevins talks good Spanish. The kid said that Mrs. Ramirez wanted to see you. He led her burro, but they ended up at my place, where Norma fed 'em both, and then started for your place, takin' the old Mexican woman in the buckboard. That's all he knows. Sing Low knew almost that much. He said the old lady told Norma a lot of stuff, but he didn't know what it was.'

'Grandma Ramirez!' exclaimed Micky. 'Now, what in hell would bring her up here?'

'Do you know her pretty well?' asked Harper.

'I shore do. She's as straight as an angel.'

'I never trusted Mexicans,' said Frenchy Allard.

'You could do a damn sight worse some- times,' retorted Micky.

'But what's it all about?' asked the sheriff.

'Norma takes the old Mexican woman down to Micky's place, where that tenderfoot is stayin' alone tonight. Micky says there's buckboard tracks in the yard. The tenderfoot is gone, and the buckboard never came back.'

'Topete?' questioned Allard. 'Knowin' we was after him—'

'He shot and robbed Ross—and murdered Ted Byers,' said a cowboy.

'Great heavens, we've got to do somethin'!' blurted Harper.

'There's somethin' that looks like blood-spatter on our porch,' said Spook. 'Mebbe it ain't, but it shore looks like blood to me.'

Flint Harper's face turned gray in the yellow lamplight.

'Blood?' he said huskily. 'Is it blood, Davis?'

'I'm afraid it is, Harper.'

'We've got to find her,' muttered Flint Harper. 'We've—listen to me! I'll give five thousand dollars in cash for Norma's return alive and unhurt.'

'Five thousand!' snapped Micky. 'With all the money you've got—and you offer a measly five thousand. Damn it, I'll give anybody my whole ranch for her safe return.'

'Includin' the mortgage?' asked Duncan Wheeler.

Smack! Micky smashed Wheeler full in the mouth, and the owner of the Box JB bounced off the bar and went sprawling on the floor. He was knocked cold, his front teeth loosened by the impact of Micky's hard right fist.

'Has anybody else got a smart remark to make?' asked Micky coldly.

'Take it easy, Micky,' advised the sheriff. 'I don't reckon Dunc realized how that would sound. Everybody excited—that-a-way.'

Duncan Wheeler was getting to his feet, spitting blood and wrath, as he clumsily pawed at the butt of his gun. Apparently he was too badly dazed to realize what he was doing.

The sheriff took his gun. Micky backed against the bar, and Spook moved in beside him. The bartender brought water and a towel.

'Everybody excited—that-a-way,' repeated the sheriff.

'We've got to do somethin',' insisted Flint Harper.

'Find the tracks of that buckboard,' said Joe Nevins. 'See where it went.'

'You can't find 'em at night,' said Skee Harris. 'We can't do a damn thing until daylight.'

'They won't prove anythin',' said Micky grimly. 'You don't suppose we'll find Norma at the end of them tracks, do you? Have a little sense, Skee. Me and Spook are goin' home. At daylight we'll trail from my place—for all the good it'll do. C'mon, Spook.'

'I'll get you for this, Davis,' gritted Duncan Wheeler, shoving the wet towel aside.

'Cut your wolf loose any time you feel like it,' replied Micky, as he and Spook walked out of the saloon.

They flung themselves into their saddles and rode wearily back to the ranch. Micky was not in a conversational mood, and for once in his life Spook did not jest. The world had become a serious place. They fed their horses in the corral, then sat down in the main room for a few minutes.

'If we only knew why Grandma Ramirez wanted to see me!' said Micky. 'She came all the way up here on a burro. At her age, too. Spook, she had a message for us—somethin' damned important. I don't know how to figure Topete in this deal, unless he came to get even with Orville and ran into Norma and the old lady.'

'Or,' suggested Spook, 'she had somethin' to tell that Topete didn't want told. Mebbe she'd told Norma and Orville, and he *had* to grab all of 'em. But where could he take 'em in that buckboard?'

'Take 'em in a buckboard? Spook, a buckboard is plenty flexible. Why, I'll betcha I could take a buckboard and a bronc team and go plumb across the border without tippin' over once. Topete knows every inch of this border, knows everythin' about the country between here and the border. If he wanted to take 'em down there in a buckboard, he could do it.'

'Yeah, I s'pose he could, Micky. Only I'm arguin' that he didn't.'

'I hope not. Mexico is awful wide and long. It would take me a long time to run him down—in Mexico.'

'Would yuh try it, Micky?'

'He's got Norma,' replied Micky simply.

'That's right.'

Micky took the cigarette from between his lips, his eyes staring at the blank wall. He blinked thoughtfully.

'Norma never came out here, before,' he said. 'I wonder if Grandma Ramirez told her that she was the one that got the presents from me. Could that be why she brought the old lady out here? No, that don't sound reasonable. Grandma wouldn't ride a mule all the way up here just to tell Norma that.'

'Must be somethin' more important than that,' said Spook.

'There's nothin' more important—to me, Spook.'

'Yeah, I reckon that's right. Love's a funny thing.'

'Topete was sore at Orville 'cause he busted in on him at the Harper ranch and made him let Norma alone. Mebbe he came here to get Orville and—but if he wanted to kill Orville why ain't the body around here?'

'Don't talk about bodies bein' around here,'

wailed Spook. 'Mebbe it's in the buckboard. When we find that buckboard—'

'Don't worry about that buckboard,' said Micky. 'It won't help any. They're a long ways from that buckboard right now. Well, mebbe we better try to grab a little shut-eye; it'll soon be mornin'.'

XII
A Way Out

At daylight every available rider around Encinitas was out on the road. Micky and Spook searched both sides, until they met several more searchers coming from Encinitas. They found where the wheel-prints left the road south of Encinitas, circled the town, and came back into the road beyond. They were trailing when Flint Harper and his men came from the north. About a mile from Pancho's Place they found the buckboard and team tied at the side of the road.

There were blood spots on the cushions of the buckboard, too. There were no trails in that vicinity; no way even to guess which way the people had gone. Pancho Ortega, owner of Pancho's Place, swore that neither Topete nor anyone else had been there last night, except the driver of the stage. A sleepy-eyed bartender attested to this.

Duncan Wheeler, his lips split and swollen, was in the posse, along with Frenchy Allard and 'Big Bill' Long. Bill was not feeling well, but insisted on going with them. Nothing more was said about Micky's knocking Duncan Wheeler down at the Smoke Tree Saloon, but Micky felt that the issue was not settled yet.

After investigating Pancho Ortega they all rode back to Encinitas, each man trying to puzzle out what to do next. The town was aroused over the disappearance of Norma Harper. The name of Topete was on every lip. Some suggested going back to Topete's place.

'A waste of time,' declared Micky. 'There's been two trips down to Topete's rancho. He's too smart to stay there.'

'He must have taken them to Mexico,' said the sheriff. 'Mebbe he didn't take 'em to his rancho, but they're down there, I'll bet.'

'There's plenty hidin' places in Mexico,' said Bill Long.

'There's plenty hidin' places in Arizona too,' declared the sheriff. 'I believe we stand a lot better chance of findin' somebody if we scatter out. As a posse, we can only go one place at a time.'

'That's my idea,' agreed Micky. 'C'mon, Spook.'

'Wait a minute!' snorted the sheriff. 'Tell us where you're goin', so none of us will be covering that same country.'

'Don't bother about us, Buck,' replied Micky. 'I'm not advertisin' my plans. C'mon, Spook.'

They rode south, as though going back to their ranch, but cut back and circled wide of the town. Spook did not ask any questions until they were far out in the rocky hills, toward Lobo Solo Canyon, when he said:

'Now, what's your hunch, Micky?'

'No hunch in the world, except that somebody out here had a reason to shoot Ted Byers. It looks as though Ted ran into Topete, and Topete shot him. That part of it is plain enough, but what was Topete doin' out here?'

'Goin' like hell, the last you seen of him,' remarked Spook.

'That's right. But Topete might have a hangout along the canyon. He's keepin' away from his rancho, and he's got to have a place to stay.'

They reached the spot where they had heard the shot fired. Here they dismounted, and began searching carefully, leading their horses. The mesquite was like barbed-wire entanglements, making travel very slow and difficult. They smashed through thickets of sage and catclaw, not to mention a dozen different species of cactus.

Micky, working in close to the rim of the canyon, made a discovery—a rutted cattle trail into the canyon, visible for about thirty feet, where it dipped in around a pinnacle of rocks. He called to Spook, who left his horse and crawled through the brush. There were horse tracks in the trail, too.

'That's somethin' to look at,' said Spook quietly.

'A trail into Lobo Solo,' said Micky. 'And a mighty well hid trail, too. We'll hide our horses and take a walk down there.'

'All right, cowboy; I believe you've found what we've been lookin' for.'

They led their horses up along the rim, where they concealed them behind a heavy screen of mesquite far from the trail. Then they went back and started to descend. The trail twisted to the left under the pinnacle of rock, where it was so narrow that a rider would have to lean out over the depths to prevent the rocks from knocking him out of the saddle.

It pitched steeply to another level, where it crowded in against a cliff and was little more than a series of sandstone ledges. They halted in against the shade of a cliff and peered into the canyon, but could see nothing. They were carrying their ropes, looped over a shoulder, their holstered guns swinging handy.

Down they went into the cool depths, marveling that anyone had ever discovered this means of getting into inaccessible Lobo Solo's north end, and finally arrived at the sandy bottom, brushy and rocky. Here the bottom of the trail was blocked with several poles.

The rim of the canyon seemed very far away, and there was only a narrow sweep of blue sky—very blue from down there. They were cautious now, working their way carefully. Here was water, muddy from hoofs, but flowing slowly from springs.

Then they ran into yearlings—unbranded stock.

'My yearlin's!' exclaimed Micky. 'They shoved the bunch down here, holdin' 'em for a brandin', knowin' that we'd never look for a way into Lobo Solo. Now, if we can only find out who did it, Spook.'

They found the cave where Orville had been held. There was canned food stacked against the rocky wall, empty tins scattered around, the remnants of a cooking-fire, and extra wood. In a far corner were two bed rolls, and tucked under the rope on one roll was a Winchester .30-30, with a beltful of cartridges.

Micky took the gun and examined it. It was nearly new, with no marks to show ownership. The magazine was filled. Micky pumped a shell into the chamber and dropped the rifle into the crook of his arm, after he had fastened the belt around his waist.

'This might be a big help,' he remarked. 'Now the question is—do we try and haze this bunch of yearlin's up that trail and out on the rim, on foot, or do we wait here until the gentlemen return and give 'em hell?'

'I vote to give 'em hell,' replied Spook. 'I shore don't want to hop around this canyon on high heels chasin' yearlin's. It's a cinch they can't get away, so let's camp right here.'

'I want to notch this .30-30 on Topete, Spook, but worse than that I want to find Norma and Red. We know where the yearlin's are now; and we know that Norma and Red ain't down here. Let's go back. I'll shove this gun into the bed roll so they won't know we've been here. This will keep. Hell, they've got a big brandin' job ahead of 'em, and I'd like to get 'em red-handed.'

'Suits me,' said Spook. 'This place don't appeal to me. I never did like to be down in a hole with only one way out. Too much like a trap.'

Micky went back and replaced the rifle. Spook was standing at the entrance, looking back toward the trail up the walls, two hundred yards away, when a rifle bullet smashed into the sandstone only a few inches from his face. It sprayed rock dust into his face, and he fell backward into the mouth of the cave, clawing at his eyes.

Micky grabbed the rifle and ran out to Spook.

'Glory be, are you hurt?' he asked anxiously. Spook jerked himself farther into the cave.

'Damn bullet threw sand in my face!' he wailed. 'Where'd it come from?' Spook sat up and wiped his tear-filled eyes.

Micky peered around the corner, and another bullet flipped past him, whining off the rocks beyond the cave.

'Somebody shootin' from the trail,' he said, risking another look.

'Trapped,' wailed Spook. 'Only one way out—and they're standin' on it.'

'I can't see a soul,' declared Micky. He picked up a long stick, placed Spook's hat on it, and cautiously raised it above the rock.

Pwee-e-e-e! A bullet ripped through the crown of the hat and went smashing into the rocky wall. Micky lowered the hat and showed it to Spook.

'Pretty good shootin',' he remarked calmly.

Spook grabbed the hat and jerked it down on his head.

'That's a hell of a thing to do—use *my* hat!' he complained.

'Do you know that we ain't in such a bad spot?' said Micky. 'They can't get behind us. If they try to circle that other wall we can shore make 'em hard to catch. All we've got to do is take it easy and let them come to us.'

'What about darkness?' asked Spook.

'No advantage to them. In fact, we've got the best of it, 'cause we're already here. We can lay still—and they can't. I don't mind the situation a little bit, except that it keeps us here.'

'Yea-a-a-h! And all they've got to do is guard that damn trail. We can't stay here forever, you know.'

'Of course there are drawbacks,' admitted Micky.

There had been no shots for fifteen or twenty minutes. Micky exposed his own hat, but with no results. A bunch of the yearlings went past, going to the water hole.

'We can shore eat meat,' he told Spook. The light was getting poor as the sun sank in the west. The whole canyon was in shadow now. Micky leaned against the rocky wall, his eyes narrowed as he looked at the rocky walls, wondering just where that trail ran along. Suddenly he grunted softly and lifted the rifle to his shoulder.

Far up the side of the wall, at least four hundred yards away, a horse and rider were going up the trail, barely visible against the rocky wall. Micky cuddled the gun against his shoulder, guessed at the needed elevation, and squeezed the trigger. Spook leaning close, saw the horse lose its stride when the bullet whined close.

Micky quickly levered in another cartridge, and again the canyon rattled from the report of the .30-30. But this shot brought plenty of action. They saw the horse stagger and go down on the trail. Then it turned over the edge, hurtled into space, and came down into the canyon, end over end.

But the rider had fallen on the upper side of the trail. They saw him get to his feet, clawing his way up the trail, a tiny figure. Micky sent three more shots in his direction before he disappeared around a corner of rock. The horse had crashed to a brushy ledge, fifty feet above the bottom of the canyon.

Micky quickly stuffed cartridges into the loading-gate of the rifle.

'It wasn't the palomino,' said Spook.

'Nope. But I set that snake-hunter on foot. What a lucky shot! Well, mebbe the trail is open, Spook.'

Spook stepped out, and a bullet missed his head by an inch. He promptly fell back behind the rock again.

'The trail ain't open, Mr. Davis,' he said weakly.

'It seems to be decidedly closed, Mr. Sullivan,' agreed Micky.

They sat down and rolled smokes.

'I'll tell you what we'll do,' said Micky. 'As soon as it gets plenty dark we'll separate and start our advance on the bottom of the trail. Between the two of us, we ought to get that whippoorwill.'

'Thank you kindly, Mr. Davis, but I think I'll stay right here. He's prob'ly in a right nice place to spray us both. I'm jest like an Apache—don't like to fight in the dark. Night was made for sleepin', anyway.'

'You ain't gettin' scared, are you, Spook?'

'*Gettin'* scared? Why, I've been white as a sheet for an hour.'

More yearlings drifted past, going to water.

'Dogies are gittin' mighty thin,' observed

Spook. 'Ain't much food down here. Another few weeks and they'd be too weak to climb the hill.'

'You know, Spook, this situation don't look so good for us. There's only one way out of here. One man could keep us in here for the rest of our days. One of us should have stayed at the top.'

'If we don't show up for a couple days somebody will be lookin' for us, Micky.'

'Lookin' for us in the bottom of Lobo Solo? Don't be foolish.'

'Micky,' said Spook soberly, 'didja ever see a man who was plumb panic-stricken?'

'I don't reckon I ever have, Spook.'

'Well, you're goin' to see one, if you don't quit pointin' out that we're trapped down here. I'm an optimist.'

'Even an optimist can't fly, Spook. Peek out and see if that rifle-shooter is still on the job.'

'Why me?' queried Spook.

'You're the optimist of this party.'

'Yeah, I know, but it don't do to carry a thing like that too far.'

Darkness comes swiftly in the desert country, especially in a deep canyon, where there is only a narrow strip of sky to furnish light. A chill wind swept past the cave where Spook and Micky crouched, several feet apart. Finally, Micky went back into the cave, opened the bed rolls, and secured a couple of blankets.

Suddenly a yearling bawled queerly, and there was a clattering of hoofs as a bunch of the young cattle scattered. The yearling bawled again—a muffled, choked bawl.

'There goes twenty dollars,' said Micky.

'What was it?' whispered Spook nervously.

'Mountain lion.'

'Gosh!' gasped Spook. 'A lion down here? Well, if a lion can get out of here, I can.'

'Mebbe he can't,' said Micky.

Another hour passed. The tip of a crescent moon showed over the rim of the canyon. Spook threw his blanket aside and got to his feet.

'I'll tell you about me,' he said firmly. 'In the daylight we ain't got a burglar's chance to go over that trail—if anybody is watchin' for us. You can stay here if you want to, Micky—but I'm goin' out.'

'Mebbe yo're right, Spook. I want to get out as badly as you do.'

Micky threw his blanket aside and picked up his rope.

'We might as well keep together,' he said. 'No use shootin' at each other in the dark.'

They stepped out into the canyon, only a few feet away from the cave, when there was a sheet of flame from the canyon wall, illuminating the cliffs, and a heavy explosion seemed to shake the earth.

'My gosh, what was that?' blurted Spook. The

thunder of the explosion died away, and the canyon was very quiet when Micky replied:

'I reckon we can sleep in peace, Spook; somebody has dynamited the trail.'

'You mean—we're trapped, Micky?'

'Well, you didn't think they were firin' a salute in our honor, did you?'

'But—but this loses all them yearlin's for them, Micky.'

'Yeah, that's true,' agreed Micky, 'but it prob'ly saves their damn necks. Let's dig out them bed rolls; we might as well be comfortable.'

Neither of them slept much until about dawn, when Spook's snores attested to the fact that he had forgotten their predicament. Micky, unable to sleep, sat up in his blankets, pondering over the situation. The sky indicated daylight, but the canyon was still in semidarkness, when a deer, like a gray shadow, passed within a hundred feet of him. It was an old doe, followed in a few moments by a younger doe, and finally by a big buck. They were going to the water hole.

Micky started to rouse Spook, but decided to wait a few minutes. It was barely possible that these three deer had reached the canyon bed over the same trail that Micky and Spook had used; but Micky did not believe this.

The three deer drank their fill and came back. This time the wind had changed, and they got the man scent, stopped, and lifted their big ears, as they sniffed the tainted breeze. After a few moments they went on, walking jerkily, heads held high. Micky got quietly to his feet and followed, keeping in close to the rocky wall.

The deer walked in single file, apparently little alarmed. About a mile north of the cave, they turned abruptly to the left, went through a thicket, and were out of sight. Micky hurried now. Just before he reached the thicket he glanced up at the wall beyond, and saw the three deer traveling along a trail on the side of the cliffs. He stood and watched them out of sight. He wanted to throw his hat in the air and cheer. The deer had showed him another trail out of the canyon. When Micky returned, Spook was still asleep, but he sat up quickly and rubbed his eyes.

'Where you been?' he asked.

'Chasin' three deer out of the canyon,' replied Micky.

'Chasin' three deer—*out* of the canyon? Out where?'

'About a mile above here—out the east side, Spook. It can't be a bad trail, 'cause they came down here to get water. And where a deer can go—we can take them yearlin's.'

'To hell with the yearlin's!' snorted Spook. 'All I care about is this: is it a trail where old man Sullivan's favorite son can get a toehold?'

'You can walk on a deer trail, can't you? Throw

them blankets into the cave and let's be travelin', before I forget the place to start climbin'.'

They took a can of salmon and a can of tomatoes from the stock in the cave. Micky carried the rifle. No telling what they might meet before they could circle the head of the canyon and reach their horses—if they were still where they had left them.

The deer trail was well concealed. In fact, there was no trail until they worked their way through a short, brushy side canyon. There the trail began. It was narrow but hard-packed, and followed a long slant far up the canyon, where it doubled back at an easy grade. It was at least twice as long as the other trail, but with no hard climbs nor dangerous spots, except that a misstep would send one down into the depths.

They came out of the canyon about a mile from the north end, into a twenty-acre thicket of mesquite, where there were no trails. But that was simple traveling for the two cowboys. They breathed a sigh of thanksgiving when they stepped over the rim.

'I'm cured on deer-huntin',' declared Spook. 'I'll never shoot one again—unless he's goin' for me.'

'Same here,' smiled Micky. 'You can see why nobody ever found the down trail from this side. You'd never think of searchin' through a thicket like this. And you'd have to crawl the edge to find it. We can sure take them yearlin's out this way, Spook.'

'That's right. I wonder what's goin' on in Encinitas.'

'We better be travelin',' said Micky. 'I sure hope there'll be a lot of good news for us.'

Because of the nature of the country, it required fully three hours for Micky and Spook to circle the canyon and get back to their horses. No one had found them. But Micky was curious about the dynamited trail, and decided to go down far enough to see how badly it had been damaged.

'Not me,' declared Spook. 'I'm never goin' to let them whippoorwills get in above me again. You can go down, while I watch the top of the trail.'

That was satisfactory with Micky.

'We better go mighty careful,' he warned. 'You never can tell what might happen.'

Cautiously they circled the brush and approached the rim. Suddenly Micky jerked to a stop. A man stepped out of the brush, twenty feet away, swinging up a sixshooter. His first shot, fired too quickly, missed Micky by a foot. It was so sudden and unexpected that Micky did not realize what was happening until the next shot tugged at his left sleeve.

Then Micky drew and fired. The man jerked sideways, recovered his balance, and lifted his gun again; but Micky's second shot was deliberate, with no possibility of a miss. The man went to his knees, swayed for a moment, then sprawled forward on his face.

'Holy Mike!' exploded Spook. 'You sure sealed his earthly envelope, Micky!'

Cautiously, they approached the man and turned him over on his back.

'Manuel Ramirez!' exclaimed Micky. 'What in the devil—'

The Mexican—son of Grandma Ramirez—was not a pretty sight. His head was swollen from an unhealed, untended scalp laceration. The left sleeve of his shirt, torn off, revealed a swollen and discolored arm and shoulder; his hands were cut and bruised. His eyes flicked open, and he stared up at Micky.

'*Amigo*,' he whispered. '*Por Dios*, I make meestake.'

'You sure came within an inch of makin' one,' said Spook.

'Who was you waitin' for, Manuel?' questioned Micky, but the dying Mexican did not seem to understand. He said:

'They theenk I tell, so they try keel me. Throw me in bushes. I no keeled. I go home, get gun, and come back to keel. *Por—Dios—*the—dark! *Amigo*—I—mak'—meestake.'

Micky reached up slowly and removed his hat.

'We all make mistakes, Manuel,' he said.

'In your condition, I reckon we can excuse you.'

'Sure,' added Spook. 'You wasn't to blame, feller.'

'I guess we're talkin' to a dead man,' said Micky quietly. 'Let's search around and see if we can find his horse; so we can take him to Encinitas. I sure hate to have to tell Grandma Ramirez.'

'We'll have to find her first,' reminded Spook. 'But who in the devil was he waitin' to pot-shoot, Micky?'

'*Quién sabe*? But it's a cinch that Manuel was the Mexican that Orville fought with down in the canyon. That scalp cut was prob'ly the result of that fight between 'em. It might be that they figured Manuel's worth was over, after he let Orville go; so they decided to kill Manuel and shut his mouth for keeps.'

'Manuel worked for Topete,' reminded Spook. 'Mebbe he waited for Topete.'

'My hunch is that Manuel was workin' for some Americanos on this deal. The border Mexicans would be all right if the damned Americans wouldn't make crooks out of 'em. In ninety-nine cases out of a hundred you'll find a white man payin' the Mexican. Even Topete would be all right if it wasn't for white men. He ain't got brains enough to do these things himself. If it wasn't for white men, Manuel would be down at his own place, takin' care of his goats, instead of layin' there, starin' at the sky and not seein' it.'

'I don't reckon he could help finishin' up that-a-way,' said Spook. 'It 'pears to me that folks ain't got a hell of a lot to say about how they die.'

'I don't reckon they have,' sighed Micky. 'Let's find his horse.'

A short distance away from the spot where Manuel died they found his horse tied in a thicket. They untied the animal and led it back to the body, where Micky prepared the ropes.

'If yuh ask me, I don't like this job,' declared Spook. 'Handlin' dead bodies is plumb out of my line. Gee, that poor devil shore took a beatin' from somebody.'

'From Topete, I reckon,' sighed Micky. 'It looks as though Manuel had been waitin' here to bush Topete, but missed his shot. That would account for the shot we heard. And I'd make a little bet that Manuel was the Mexican that Orville fought with. He prob'ly helped Topete steal our calves, and he knowed that Topete would come here.

'Now, I've got to go down and tell Grandma Ramirez about how I gunned up her boy. But she'll understand, don'tcha think, Spook?'

' 'Course she'll understand. She realized that Manuel was a bad boy. I reckon she tried to keep him straight.'

'I know,' nodded Micky. 'But just the same, he

was her son. Seems like a mother can stand for a lot from their own kid. Mine did.'

'You lift him up and I'll juggle the ropes,' said Spook. 'If I had t' do it I'd be wakin' up nights for a month, breakin' out in cold sweats. Didja ever have a cold sweat, Micky?'

'Not too cold,' grunted Micky, as he lifted the body.

XIII

Reward!

There were many riders in Encinitas that day. Except for Micky and Spook, all the searchers were back in town, wondering where to go next. There were extra riders from Sierra Vista, who had come in to assist in the search. Among them were 'Shorty' Boland, Ike Akers, and Jud Moran, the men who had drunk with Orville in Sierra Vista.

'I don't know Miss Harper none,' stated Shorty, 'but we shore do sabe that red-headed feller. He's a pretty good singer, but he ain't worth shucks as a drinker. We're in here to he'p find the boy.'

Flint Harper was offering ten thousand dollars for Norma, alive and unharmed, while the county offered two thousand, dead or alive, for Topete, with Ed Ross's five hundred added. Sleepy-eyed cowboys lounged around the bar at the Smoke Tree Saloon, while the sheriff, Flint Harper, and Duncan Wheeler conferred on what to do next.

'I wish Micky Davis and Spook Sullivan would show up,' said the sheriff.

'Are you havin' a meetin' with the commissioners this mornin'?' asked Wheeler.

'That's right,' nodded the sheriff. 'The prosecutin' attorney will be there, too. My idea is to boost that reward money at least five thousand dollars. Fifteen thousand dollars will keep the cowpunchers workin' night and day. We're pretty sure that if we can find Topete we'll find Norma, Woodruff, and the old Mexican woman.'

'If he's holdin' 'em for ransom, why in hell don't he ask for it?' said Harper wearily. 'He knows I'll pay. The trouble is,' said Harper, 'we've been figurin' him as bein' ignorant. He's smarter than hell—smarter than we are, that's a cinch. It's goin' to take brains to find him. All the riders in the State won't do us any good unless there's a brain behind 'em.'

'That counts me out,' said the sheriff soberly.

'Counts all of us out, as far as that goes,' said Wheeler grimly.

There was a commotion out in the street. Someone called to the sheriff, and the three men hurried out. Micky and Spook had arrived, with the body of Manuel Ramirez roped to his saddle.

'We ran onto him out near Lobo Solo,' stated Micky. 'He started throwin' lead at us, and I had to cut down on him.'

'Who is he, Micky?' asked the sheriff.

'Manuel Ramirez. He's the son of the old lady who disappeared with Norma and Woodruff.'

'One of Topete's henchmen, eh?' said Wheeler.

'I believe he has worked for Topete,' answered Micky.

They unroped the body and placed it in a vacant storeroom near the saloon. Harper was standing near the doorway.

'Any news?' asked Micky.

Harper shook his head wearily. 'None,' he replied shortly.

The sheriff walked down the street with Micky, questioning him about the shooting of Manuel Ramirez. But Micky told him nothing of their experiences in Lobo Solo Canyon. He merely said that he and Spook had searched all night, finally running into Manuel.

'He'd been hurt pretty bad before I shot him, Buck,' said Micky. 'He's had a fight. Have the doctor look him over. You fellers haven't found anythin'?'

'Not a damn thing.'

'How does Flint Harper feel about it?'

'He's jest about crazy. Just between me and you, Micky, who was this Mexican waitin' to shoot?'

'He didn't live long enough to tell us, Buck.'

'Was he expectin' somebody out there?'

'I'll tell you what I think, Buck; he was pretty badly busted up by somebody. Mebbe his mind wasn't workin' just right. In fact, I don't believe he knew what he was doin' when he shot at us.'

'Did he recognize you afterward?'

'Yeah, he did. He said it was a mistake. But

he didn't live to tell us who he was layin' for.'

The sheriff nodded soberly. After a few moments he said:

'You was across Lobo Solo last night, I believe you said.'

'That's right, Buck.'

'Me and Skee was out past Pancho's Place. I dunno what time it was. Mebbe long about nine, ten o'clock, we heard a blast. I wondered if you heard it.'

'Yeah, we heard it, Buck. Pretty heavy shot, too. But we couldn't quite place it. Prob'ly some prospector firin' a late load.'

'I s'pose it was. Shucks, this job has got us all kinda jumpy.'

'That's right. I notice we've got some extra help from Sierra Vista.'

'Yeah. But I feel just like Flint Harper does; we need brains more than brawn. All we've done so far is to ride the legs off our horses. That don't pay, Micky.'

'It's kinda queer—Flint Harper askin' for brains. He's always had an idea that he was pretty damn smart. But he's like a lot of other smart men, Buck. In a pinch, they lose their minds.'

'I don't reckon I had any to lose,' said the sheriff. 'Harper talked about hirin' some smart detectives, but I don't believe they'd do any good, just get themselves killed, mebbe.'

'That's about all,' agreed Micky.

'What are you goin' to do now?'

'Go home and rest up for a few hours, Buck. I'm too tired to even do a small job of thinkin'. And after we're rested, I don't know where to go next.'

'Flint Harper is offerin' ten thousand for Norma,' said the sheriff. 'I'm meetin' the commissioners and the prosecutor today to see if we can't boost our reward to five thousand for Topete. Mebbe it won't help any. Duncan Wheeler thought it might, and Harper thought it would be a good idea. I dunno—'

'Yeah, it might help,' said Micky thoughtfully. 'Well, I'll get Spook and go home for a while. We'll be back this evenin'—I think.'

The sheriff went back to the saloon and joined Wheeler and Harper.

'What do you think of Micky's story?' asked Wheeler.

'Why, it's all right,' replied the sheriff. 'Anythin' wrong with it?'

'Me and Flint been talkin' things over. Micky was in love with Norma. She went out to his place. That might be an angle.'

'Not so very good,' replied the sheriff. 'Micky and Spook were here pretty quick that night. They came right on after visitin' the ranch.'

'And they couldn't have taken that buckboard,' added Harper.

'You're overlookin' Woodruff,' said Wheeler.

The sheriff squinted thoughtfully as he caressed his stubbled chin. 'Yeah, that *could* have happened.'

'And what about the old Mexican woman comin' up here to see him? And today he killed her son. Mebbe the son knew too much. Mebbe they went to meet him, instead of runnin' into him like they said. I tell you, it looks funny to me, Buck."

'Mebbe we better watch 'em,' said the sheriff.

'They wanted to search alone,' said Wheeler. 'Hell, they wouldn't even tell where they was goin'—if you remember.'

'It's worth thinkin' about, Buck,' declared Flint Harper. 'Micky Davis hates me.'

'But he loves Norma,' said the sheriff.

'I don't want you to get the wrong angle on me,' said Wheeler. 'It might look like I was tryin' to put the deadwood on Micky because he hit me. But you'll have to admit that I *could* be right.'

'It's the first sign of brains we've had,' said Harper. 'Keep on thinkin', Dunc. Heaven knows I want this settled. It's hell, I tell you.'

'I've gone about as far as I can,' admitted Wheeler. 'There's got to be somethin' to work on. We might have somebody foller 'em and see where they go. It might lead to a solution—who knows? I could have Frenchy and Bill Long trail 'em. Neither of them are very smart, but they might be able to do that job all right.'

'That's a job for me and Skee,' replied the sheriff.

'I think so too,' said Harper. 'It might cause complications if they knew Frenchy and Bill was trailin' 'em. Micky and Spook are kinda sudden, you know.'

'Go ahead,' agreed Wheeler. 'But as far as that goes, I don't reckon Micky nor Spook would hold back, even if they knew you and Skee was trailin' 'em.'

'Anyway,' said the sheriff, 'it's our job. I dunno what to make of them shootin' that Mexican. Mebbe there's more to it than we know. I'd like to know what the Mexican told 'em before he died.'

'Did he tell 'em somethin'?' asked Wheeler.

'Well, Micky said he lived long enough to tell them that he made a mistake. I've got a feelin' that Micky's holdin' somethin' back.'

'He might be, at that,' said Wheeler. 'Anyway, you better keep an eye on them two, Buck. I reckon we'll ride back to the ranch and have supper. Bill Long ain't feelin' very good yet.'

'I'll watch 'em,' promised the sheriff.

Micky and Spook rode slowly back to the ranch. Micky was quiet and thoughtful during the ride, and when they reached the ranch, he insisted on leaving their horses down in the willows, behind the burned stable. They removed the bridles and gave the horses a feed of oats before going up to the ranch house.

'I dunno what this is all about,' said Spook, 'but it's all right.'

'It's just a hunch,' replied Micky. 'I've been thinkin' about us bringin' Manuel's body to Encinitas. Manuel was workin' for somebody who thought they had killed him off; they might suspect that Manuel told us somethin' before he died. If they should—me and you are settin' on a box of dynamite right now.'

'Gosh!' grunted Spook nervously. 'You're makin' me as jumpy as a flea in Death Valley. Mebbe we should have left him where he fell.'

'Our skin would be a lot safer if we had, agreed Micky, as they went into the ranch house.

Micky started a fire, put on the coffee-pot, and in a few minutes they were enjoying a meal of bacon and eggs and gulping big cups of hot coffee. It was their first meal in twenty-four hours, and they did justice to it.

It was midafternoon when they finished cleaning up the dishes.

'Do we go back to Encinitas?' asked Spook.

'We do not,' replied Micky. 'We're goin' to dig out our bed rolls, Spook.'

Fifteen minutes later they were down in the willows near the two horses, where they spread their beds in the shade.

'This is a hell of an idea,' complained Spook.

'I know it,' agreed Micky. 'But I've got a hunch that we might have company tonight, and I don't want to be in that house. But I do want to be close enough to see if I can find out who wants to see us. If you want to stay in the house go ahead; I'll do what I can for you.'

'Thank you very much, Mr. Davis,' said Spook soberly, as he stretched out on his blankets, 'but I always did have a hankerin' to keep my own skin as intact as possible. Call me when the company comes. I'm takin' on a little shut-eye. I never do sleep well in a canyon.'

'Go ahead,' advised Micky. 'I filled a lamp and lighted it so they'll think we're home. It'll burn until midnight, I reckon.'

Buck Bramer had no liking for shadowing Micky and Spook, but since Duncan Wheeler and Flint Harper had voiced their suspicions, Buck felt that it was his duty to keep an eye on the two Bar D cowboys. Buck explained it to Skee, whose only comment was:

'Suits me all right; I'm a good waiter.'

They expected that Micky and Spook would be back at Encinitas before dark. Buck had told Harper and Wheeler that he and Skee would take up their shadowing work as soon as Micky and Spook came back. But when darkness came and the two men did not come back, Buck decided to go out to the Bar D, without telling anyone that he and Skee were leaving town.

They rode quietly away. About a mile from the ranch house they left the road and cut across the hills, coming in at the rear of the place. There was a light in the ranch house. They left their horses in a secluded place, and approached the house on foot.

'We'll work in close enough to take a peek into the house,' explained the sheriff. 'If they're home, we'll just hang around and see if they pull out, then foller 'em.'

'Be damn careful about the peekin',' said Skee. 'I know them two jaspers well enough to know that they'll shoot first and ask questions afterward. And you better do the peekin', Buck, 'cause I get sinkin' spells when anybody shoots at me.'

They came in on the opposite side from where Micky and Spook were watching the house. The sheriff crawled in close and peered into the main room. Skee crouched near him. For ten or fifteen minutes they watched and listened.

'Queer deal,' muttered the sheriff. 'Nobody in sight and not a damn sound. If they went away, why did they leave a lamp burnin'?'

'Mebbe they're tryin' to fool somebody,' suggested Skee.

'Wouldn't be tryin' to fool us. They don't know we're watchin' 'em.'

'I hope not.'

'All right. This window is loose, Skee. We're

goin' in and stay right there for a while. Anyway, I want to look this place over. C'mon.'

'Well, I reckon I'm paid to help you make mistakes, Buck. I feel like a damn burglar. I tell you, I don't like it.'

'We're the law, Skee.'

'Yeah, I know; but that fact never bullet-proofed anybody. You always say, "The law's behind us." That's fine. If the law wasn't so damn porous, I'd a lot rather have it front of me. A rock or a stump or a hole in the ground is worth a hell of a lot more to me than the law, in a time of stress. But go ahead; I'm with you, Buck.'

They crawled through a window, and in order to not be too conspicuous they crawled from room to room. The house was empty. They came back to the main room and sat against the wall near a corner. After about fifteen minutes of waiting, Skee whispered:

'Just what alibi are you goin' to give Micky and Spook when they come home? Have you thought up a reason for me and you to be settin' here in their ranch house? You can't tell 'em that you got in here by mistake and didn't have brains enough to get out.'

'That's right,' sighed Buck. 'It would look queer to them.'

'I hope to tell you it'd look queer. Anyway, you said we was goin' to foller 'em and see where they went. Any danged fool would know that they'd e-ventually come back home. They're gone. Them a-comin' back home wouldn't be any evidence against 'em.'

'Yeah, that's right, Skee.'

'Well, let's get to hell out of here before they come back.'

'All right, all right. I don't like this any better than you do.'

They got to their feet, and Skee headed for the front door.

'I ain't goin' to crawl through no damned winders again,' he declared.

Skee flung the door open, and they both stepped out on the little front porch. From not over a hundred feet away, twin streams of flame lashed out in the darkness. Bullets thudded into the house, the lamp was smashed, as shot after shot tore into the darkness of the porch corner.

Buck Bramer dived off the porch, landing in a heap near the corner of the house, while Skee Harris promptly fell backward through the doorway. At least a dozen bullets smashed into the doorway, or through the open doorway, thudding into the walls of the main room.

It was over in a few seconds. Then they heard running feet, fading off in the distance. Buck Bramer sat up, panting heavily. The fall had knocked the breath out of him. He called shakily:

'Skee! Oh, Skee!'

'Yeah?' called Skee weakly from inside the house.

'Hurt?' asked Buck anxiously.

'Bumped my damn head,' complained Skee. 'Who was it?'

'How'd I know who it was? Hell, I fell off the porch and knocked all the wind out of me.'

'Did they get away?'

'Well, I—I hope so,' replied the sheriff.

Skee came crawling out and slid off the porch.

'I fell backward and hit my damn head on a chair,' he explained.

'Lucky we didn't get all shot to hell,' said the sheriff. 'I don't see how they missed us, danged if I do.'

'You ain't complainin', are you?' queried Skee. 'I think one of them bullets burned a blister on the end of my nose as I was fallin'. Man, they came through that doorway like a nest of hornets.'

The sheriff sighed deeply. 'I dunno, Skee. Mebbe it was Micky and Spook, but I hate to believe it.'

'Mebbe,' suggested Skee, 'it was somebody who mistook us for Micky and Spook.'

'Yeah, that might be true. Let's go home. Hell, I've had enough of this kinda work.'

They went back to their horses and rode to Encinitas, thankful to be alive and unhurt.

XIV

Not Shooting Square

The shooting came as a complete surprise to Micky and Spook. They did not know that the sheriff and deputy had climbed through a window. It was too dark for them to have seen the attacking party. One moment everything was quiet and serene, and the next moment it was like a battle.

It began and finished too quickly for either of them to make any move. They heard the mumble of voices beside the porch, but were unable to understand what was being said, or who was talking. Then they heard the two men moving away, and heard the creak of barbed wire as they crawled through a fence on the other side of the house.

'I'll be a blood brother to a bug!' snorted Spook.

'It seems to me,' said Micky quietly, 'that two factions used our place as a battlefield. Who it was and what it was all about, I'll be darned if I can figure out, Spook.'

'It strikes me,' said Spook, 'that both outfits wanted our scalps, and fought over 'em, before they collected.'

'Maybe you're right at that,' agreed Micky. 'Let's take a chance and find out what damage they done. Mebbe we can collect a dead man or two. Somebody should have stopped one of them bullets.'

'Do you reckon it's safe?' asked Spook.

'I reckon so. Sounded to me as though both sides pulled out.'

They went carefully to the house. The front door was wide open, the lamp smashed. They drew the window shades and lighted another lamp. Bullets had scored the top of the table. One went through the back of a rocking-chair, and two of them bored holes through the stovepipe in the kitchen.

'Man, that doorway must have been full of lead!' exclaimed Spook.

Micky lighted a lantern and went out in the yard. He had little trouble locating the spot where the shooters had stood. There were eleven empty .30-30 cartridge shells. He picked them up and went back to the house. Dumping them on the table, he examined them closely.

'Lookin' for the owner's name?' asked Spook.

'You never can tell,' said Micky.

After an inspection he pocketed two of the brass hulls, then put the lantern away.

'Hey! What's this?' exclaimed Spook, picking up a battered hat from under the rocking-chair.

On the sweatband were the initials S. H.

'Skee Harris!' exclaimed Spook. 'I recognize that old hat. But what in hell were officers doin' in here?'

'That's shore queer,' admitted Micky. 'Skee Harris. By golly, I wonder if it was Buck Bramer and Skee Harris.'

'There's how they came in!' snorted Spook, pointing at the open window. We left that winder shut.'

'Sneakin' in on us, eh?' said Micky. 'Spook, do you suppose that they suspect us? Why, that's so damn—wait a minute; I've got a hunch. They must suspect us, or they wouldn't sneak in through a window. They come here lookin' for us, sneak in the house, get tired of waitin', and—that's it! They ran into guns that were waitin' for us!'

Spook looked at him, wide-eyed in the lamp-light.

'That's it, Micky! But—but won't they think that *we* shot at 'em?'

'Holy hen hawks! Mebbe they will. Put that hat where you found it; we're pullin' out. And when we come back into Encinitas tomorrow afternoon, you'll have to admit that you forgot to blow out the lamp when we left here after supper tonight.'

'Why will I have to admit it?'

'Spook, our story has got to sound consistent. Anybody that knows you would be perfectly willin' to believe that *you* could forget to blow out a lamp.'

Leaving everything exactly as it was, Micky and Spook rode away from the ranch, cutting across the hills to Encinitas.

'Yuh never know what you'll meet on the road,' said Micky grimly. 'The more I think about this deal, the more I feel that we're suspected. If we wasn't under suspicion, why would the sheriff's office move in on us like that? If Buck Bramer and Skee Harris *was* in there, they shore will come back to look things over again, and if they find that everythin' is the same as they left it— well, it might look better for me and you.'

'Skee'll come back for his hat,' said Spook. 'He's so stingy he'd face bullets to recover that old hat. But who in hell tried to salivate them?'

'Somebody who mistook them for me and you, Spook.'

'Funny, ain't it?'

'What's funny about it?'

'The way it makes the hair kinda raise up on the back of yore neck.'

'You ought to shave the back of yore neck, Spook. I noticed the other day that you could part yore hair plumb back to yore collar.'

'Yuh couldn't part it now, 'less yuh used glue. But what are we goin' to do in town?'

'Mebbe we can find out what's goin' on.'

'You ain't aimin' to throw ourselves on the mercy of the law, are yuh, Micky?'

'Mercy of the law? Well, I hope to tell yuh I'm

not. Not after all them buckshot and bullets missed Bramer and Harris. Anyway, I never believed in the mercy of the law. I'll take my chances in the open.'

They reached town and tied their horses away from the street. Working in carefully, they looked the situation over. There were quite a number of horses at the Smoke Tree hitch rack, and they could see a number of men around the card tables in the saloon. Working in closer they could see Buck Bramer and Skee Harris. Skee was bare-headed.

'Oh, he'll go back after that hat, don'tcha worry,' said Spook.

They crossed the street in a place where there was little light and examined the horses at the hitch rack. That is, Micky did, while Spook moved in for a closer examination of the crowd inside the saloon. Micky whistled softly, and they hurried back to their horses.

'Whatcha got there—a gun?' asked Spook.

'Yeah. I borrowed one, in case somebody starts shootin' at us a long ways off.'

'Huh! That's jist like stealin' a gun, Micky.'

'It shore is similar,' chuckled Micky. 'I'll betcha there ain't a judge in Arizona who could tell the difference.'

'Could you?' queried Spook.

'If a smart judge couldn't—how can yuh expect me to do it? C'mon.'

They rode out of town in the darkness, heading directly toward Lobo Solo Canyon. Only through Micky's unerring sense of direction were they able to go there in the dark. He led the way around the head of the canyon and straight to the mesquite patch, where the hidden trail went down into the canyon.

'I hope you know where we are,' remarked Spook. 'I shore don't. I have a feelin' we're on Lobo Solo, but jist where on that damned slash in the world, I haven't any idea.'

'The deer trail is only fifty feet away,' said Micky quietly.

'Are we goin' *down* there again?'

'That's our destination, cowboy. How are yuh on a narrer trail in the dark?'

'Terrible. In fact, my father told me to never go down narrow trails in the dark. Why, you'd need a lantern, Micky. And after all, what's down there that's so wild we have to go after it in the dark?'

'I don't know,' confessed Micky. 'I'm playin' a hunch, Spook. It may not be anythin' except a fool idea. But the answer is somewhere down there—that and what I've already got.'

'All right. But if I slip it'll be too bad, 'cause I'm one of the stiffest fallers in Arizona. I jist can't relax. C'mon.'

Close behind Micky he went, both fending the mesquite limbs away with their arms crossed in front of their faces. Micky stopped short.

'Darn near stepped off,' he said. 'Here's the trail. Be careful when yuh step, and don't hurry. We've got all night to do this job, and I'd hate to have to pack yuh out of here all busted up.'

'Man, you shore paint a swell picture for me to look at. If we only had some stars! I never seen any place as dark as this.'

Slowly they went down that trail, where a misstep would send them far into the canyon. In places the rocks brushed their shoulders, but they went carefully, feeling for each step, testing it to be sure they were not on the crumbling edge.

It seemed hours before they reached that little thicket, where they were off the deer trail, and a few minutes later they were on the wide bottom of the canyon.

'I could dance and sing,' declared Spook.

'Take it easy,' advised Micky. 'Yuh can still trip over boulders and break a leg.'

Slowly they worked their way along the foot of the cliff, reaching the cave, where they rested a while and enjoyed a smoke.

'Yuh know,' mused Spook, 'I've been thinkin' about a remark that Orville made about you, Micky. It was that time I was learnin' him how to operate that sixshooter. He asked me if you was in love with Norma.'

'He did, eh?'

'Yea-a-ah. He's a queer jigger.'

'What else did he say?' asked Micky.

'Well, he said he wondered if you loved Norma, bein' as you had a girl in Mexico.'

'A girl in Mexico? Where'd he get that idea?'

'I dunno. He seemed to know that yuh had one down there.'

Micky laughed shortly. 'I wonder if Norma told him that.'

'Why would she tell him a thing like that, Micky?'

'Yuh know, Spook, I never figured out why she quit writin' to me, unless it was somethin' like that. Yuh see, she wrote and asked me if I was takin' presents to a woman in Mexico. Mebbe somebody told her I was takin' stuff to Grandma Ramirez—I dunno. I thought she was jokin'; so I wrote and told her I was. After that she never opened my letters. I wrote and told her all about it, but of course she never opened my letters—jist sent 'em back unopened.'

'I never had no luck with wimmin either,' said Spook.

'I guess it wouldn't make any difference with her, even if I did explain now,' remarked Micky.

'Why not?'

'Well—after me and her father almost shootin' each other.'

'Mebbe that's right. Girls don't like to have their fathers shot up. At least, I don't reckon they do. It ain't natural. But what are we doin' down here, Micky? It's too blamed dark to see anythin', even if there was anythin' down here.'

'Spook, do yuh remember that feller shootin' at us from over on that trail?'

'I can't even forget it in m' sleep, cowboy. The other night I was dreamin' it. I ducked a bullet and hit my head on the side of the bunk. Do I remember it!'

'We're lookin' for that place in the dark.'

'Yuh don't suppose he's still there, waitin' for us, do yuh?'

Micky laughed quietly as he peered into the darkness of the canyon.

'No, I don't believe he is, Spook; but mebbe he left somethin' I'd like to see.'

After they were rested Micky led the way through the darkness to the bottom of the trail, where he broke off some dry branches and made a torch. Moving carefully, they scanned the ground in the torchlight. It was slow work because of the lack of illumination.

'Now, if I knowed what to find,' suggested Spook meaningly.

'Rifle shells, Spook. Yuh see—oh-oh! Here we are!'

In the middle of the trail were two rifle cartridge cases, which Micky picked up and examined by the torchlight.

'If that's what brought us all the way up here, I'll be damned!' snorted Spook disgustedly. 'I thought that at least it might be a footprint of the son-of-a-gun who shot at us. But empty shells! Say, I could have found plenty of 'em right at the ranch. In fact, I've got a cigar-box full of the darned things.'

'Not like these,' grinned Micky. 'This-here pair are worth all the rest of 'em in Arizona. Wait a minute!'

Micky cocked the rifle, pointed it at the stars, and a moment later the canyon walls echoed and re-echoed from the report of the .30-30. Levering out the shell, Micky looked closely at it, chuckled again, and put the shell in a separate pocket from the others.

'All m' life,' wailed Spook, 'I've had a horror of bein' caught in a deep canyon with a lunatic.'

'Quit wavin' that torch,' said Micky. 'Mebbe it'll last to light us to the bottom of that other trail. C'mon, cowboy.'

Buck Bramer and Skee Harris went back to their office, and it was not until they reached Encinitas that Skee discovered he had lost his hat.

'I ain't goin' back to look for it,' he declared. 'I reckon I lost it when I fell back into the house.'

'Micky will find it—and wonder,' said Buck. 'He can just keep on wonderin', too; it suits me fine.'

Over at the Smoke Tree Saloon they found several riders. Duncan Wheeler and Frenchy

Allard had just arrived from their ranch. They said that Bill Long didn't feel like riding any more that day, so they had left him at the ranch to rest a while. The sheriff said nothing about being out at the Bar D.

Flint Harper and his men arrived a little later. The suspense was terrible for Flint Harper. He looked gaunt and haggard; aged years in a few hours. There was nothing arrogant about Flint Harper now.

'No news?' he asked wistfully.

'Not a thing, Flint,' replied the sheriff.

'I guess there isn't anything to do. No one knows which way to turn.'

A poker game started, but Flint Harper did not play. He and Duncan Wheeler and the sheriff sat together around a card table, trying to puzzle out what to do next.

'Davis and Sullivan didn't come in tonight?' queried Harper.

'Not yet,' replied the sheriff. 'They said they'd come back.'

'They'll bear watchin'—them two,' said Wheeler.

Flint Harper leaned across the table, looking keenly at Wheeler.

'Dunc, you told me that Micky Davis had a woman in Mexico. Where does she live?'

'I dunno,' replied Wheeler. 'Somewhere down there—mebbe at Mesquite.'

'What's her name?'

'I don't know her name. Why, Flint?'

'She might talk—about Micky. I'm wonderin' why they shot Manuel Ramirez. Could you find that woman, Dunc?'

'I don't know.'

'Dunc, do you know there is a woman down there—a woman that Micky went to see?'

Wheeler laughed shortly. 'Hell, it's common knowledge that he bought presents here and took 'em down there. A man don't buy geegaws for men. He bought 'em pretty often, I understand.'

'I see. You led me to understand that you knew who the woman was.'

'No, I didn't mean it that way, Flint. I didn't know her. Micky told Jim Gleason that he was buyin' the stuff for his sweetheart. I don't know what better evidence you'd want.'

Flint Harper sat there, leaning on the table, his eyes half-closed for several moments. Then he said wearily:

'That peon kid—he's still out there at the ranch. He told Joe Nevins that Micky bought presents for old lady Ramirez. He says that Micky Davis hasn't any girl down there.'

'That's sure funny,' said Wheeler, chuckling. 'Buyin' presents for an old lady.'

'Micky's a peculiar feller,' mused the sheriff.

'It isn't so funny,' said Harper. 'I wrote and told Norma about Micky havin' a woman in Mexico—and she quit writin' to him.'

221

'Shucks, that's too bad,' said Wheeler. 'Anyway, you don't want him in your family, Flint.'

'You don't think about things like that— ordinarily,' said Flint Harper quietly. 'No, I didn't want him, Dunc. I was glad when she stopped writin' to him. I ain't so glad now. It hurt Norma.'

'Norma's a smart girl,' said Wheeler. 'She wouldn't want to marry a feller like Micky Davis.'

'You and me, Dunc, ain't got any right to say who a girl wants to marry.'

'Well, why in the hell didn't you think of that before, Flint?'

'I guess I wasn't shootin' square with her.'

'Don't blame yourself too much, until you find out what part Micky Davis has in this deal,' said the sheriff. 'I'm not so sure he's on the square.'

Duncan Wheeler walked away to watch one of the games. Flint Harper drummed nervously on the table-top, his face grim, as he looked at the sheriff.

'In a case like this, yuh think about things, Buck,' he said soberly. 'I don't like Micky Davis. He's a hell-windin' kid, and I—I didn't think he was good enough for Norma. Mebbe she did. After all, I never asked anybody to like me when I married Norma's mother, except the woman I was goin' to marry.

'Mebbe I was pretty much of a meddlin' old fool when I wrote and told her what Dunc Wheeler said about that girl in Mexico.'

'Mebbe Dunc was doin' a little meddlin' too,' suggested the sheriff quietly.

'What do yuh mean, Buck?' queried Harper.

'Well, it might be that Dunc kinda had his eyes on her.'

Flint Harper turned his head and looked at the tall, ungainly figure of Duncan Wheeler, slightly stooped as he watched a chuck-luck game.

'I never thought about *him*,' said Flint Harper.

'Mebbe I'm wrong,' said the sheriff, 'but when a feller horns in on somethin' that ain't supposed to concern him, I allus figure he's got an axe to grind.'

'If we only knew why Norma went out to that ranch with that old Mexican woman, Buck. It would be like Norma to run right out there and make up with Micky if she knew she'd been wrong. Mebbe that was it. But that Mexican woman never came all the way from Mexico on a mule to square a deal for Micky. Anyway, she wouldn't know what it was all about.'

'It's shore a puzzle,' sighed the sheriff. 'That tenderfoot bein' missin' kinda indicates to me that Topete went out there to shoot him. When Norma and the Mexican woman showed up there—'

'If Topete wanted to kill that tenderfoot,' interrupted Harper, 'why didn't he do it, instead of takin' him away—along with the others? Why save the tenderfoot?'

'Mebbe he's got a safer place to kill him, Flint.'

'That theory don't hold water, Buck. If Topete has done all this devilment, why should he be so damn careful all to once? No, it's got more than that behind it. I figure the old Mexican woman told Norma enough to cause Norma to take her to Micky's ranch. There they ran into Topete, who knew that they knew too much; so he kidnaps all of 'em. Mebbe he listened while Norma told the tenderfoot why they came out there. Mebbe he don't want to kill 'em.'

'Well, Flint, if it hadn't been for that tenderfoot, Topete might have stolen Norma away from yore ranch that day.'

'That's true. Buck, we've got to get that dog of a Topete if it's the last thing we do.'

'And yuh might keep an eye on Micky Davis too,' remarked the sheriff. 'We can't afford to overlook anybody on this deal, Flint.'

The poker game broke up at midnight, and the players were at the bar, having a goodnight drink, when Orville Woodruff staggered into the saloon. He was dirty and unshaven; his clothes were wrinkled and torn. Both wrists were swollen, his lips puffy and sore from being bandaged.

'I'm all right,' he mumbled, as they eased him into a chair. Someone brought him a glass of whisky, another gave him cold water. The whisky choked him, but brought color to his cheeks.

'Where's Norma?' asked Harper anxiously. 'Do you know where she is?'

Orville shook his head wearily; his voice was hoarse as he replied:

'I don't know, but I—I guess she's all right.'

'Thank God for that much!' exclaimed Harper. 'Give him another shot of whisky.'

'Wait a minute!' exclaimed the sheriff. 'We don't want him drunk.'

'Where did you come from?' asked Flint Harper.

'Mexico—I guess. We rode for miles.'

'Wait a minute,' ordered the sheriff. 'We want to get this story all straight. Start at the beginnin', Woodruff.'

'It was Topete,' said Orville. 'He—he captured me at Micky's ranch, and had me all tied up, when Norma came. He hit her and knocked her down. Then he came and blindfolded me. That's the last I ever saw of her. I—I think he put me in the back of the buckboard.'

'Where did he take you?' asked the sheriff anxiously.

'I don't know. He took me out of the buckboard and left me there on the ground for a long time. Then he put me on a horse and took me away. After that ride he put me in a house, but I was blindfolded all the time. Except when he fed me, I was gagged. It was terrible.'

'Well, how the hell did you get back here—and why?'

'He came and put me on a horse, and we've been riding for miles. Then he took me off the horse, took off the ropes, and rode away. I got the blindfold and the gag off, and I could see the lights, so I managed to get here. It was terrible—trying to walk.'

'It don't make sense,' declared the sheriff. 'Why did he turn you loose, and what makes you think that Norma is all right?'

'Yes, yes; that's what we want to know,' urged Flint Harper.

'Topete is holding her for ransom,' said Orville. 'He says he can't write, so he is using me to deliver his message. He wants one hundred thousand pesos. He says to have Micky Davis bring the money to Topete's ranch at noon on Tuesday—or you'll never see Norma again. He says he trusts Micky Davis—and nobody else.'

'My God!' exclaimed Flint Harper. 'Fifty thousand dollars. Day after tomorrow is Tuesday. Why—why, I can't raise that much money; it is impossible.'

Duncan Wheeler laughed shortly. 'So he trusts Micky Davis, eh?'

The sheriff looked questioningly at Wheeler.

'Somebody would have to deliver it, Dunc,' he said.

'Shore. Micky Davis beat him up and threw him in jail—but he still trusts Micky. That's damn funny to me.'

'Can't we surround the ranch and get him?' asked one of the cowboys.

'Topete said to tell you that if anybody else except Micky came down there, the deal would be off, and Norma would not come back. He's fairly shrewd. Would you mind giving me another drink? I'm pretty well tired out, you know.'

'You shore look plenty frazzled,' admitted Skee Harris. 'But what did Topete do with the old Mexican woman?'

'Old Mexican woman? I don't believe I know anything about any old Mexican woman. He didn't say anything to me about her.'

'Do you reckon he held you at his ranch?' asked the sheriff.

'He said it wasn't his ranch. I asked him if he was one of the men who kidnaped me off the stage that night, and he just laughed and said he didn't know anything about it. I asked him if he stole Micky's calves, and he laughed again. He seemed to consider it a great joke. He said he would steal anything, if he was paid well enough.'

The bartender gave him another drink. Flint Harper plied him with more questions, but Orville had told all he knew. He wanted someone to take him out to the Bar D ranch, but they took him to the hotel, instead, so that he could get a bath.

'There's somethin' decidedly fishy about this deal,' Wheeler told Flint Harper and the sheriff. 'Topete askin' for Micky to take the money down to Mexico. I'll be damned if I'd trust him with that much money.'

'Trust him with it!' exclaimed Harper. 'Why, I can't raise it. Do you suppose that cutthroat Mexican realizes—Oh, it's out of the question. Another day and a half! Fifty thousand dollars!'

'The only other thing we can do,' said the sheriff grimly, 'is to find Norma before the time is up. I'm sheriff of this county, and the law says I can't go into Mexico. Well, all I can say is that the law can go plumb to hell in this case. We've got to outsmart Topete.'

'At least,' said Harper, 'it's encouragin' to know that she's safe for a little while.'

'He might be bluffin',' said the sheriff. 'If you only had a way of talkin' business. He's ignorant. Mebbe he don't realize that you can't raise that much money in such a short time. Hang onto your nerve, Flint.'

'I guess I'll go back to the ranch and try to sleep,' said Harper wearily. 'I'll be back in the morning.'

'I reckon we'll pull out, too,' said Duncan Wheeler. He called to Frenchy Allard, and they walked out to the hitch rack with Flint Harper.

Frenchy Allard swung into his saddle, waiting for Duncan Wheeler, who stopped for a last word with Flint Harper.

'Hey, Dunc!' called Allard. 'You didn't take the rifle out of my scabbard, didja?'

'No, I didn't, Frenchy.'

'Then somebody stole it; it's gone.'

'Maybe somebody playin' a joke on you, Frenchy.'

'I shore hope so; I paid real money for that .30-30.'

Shortly after daylight next morning, Sheriff Bramer and Skee Harris arrived at Micky's ranch house. The front door was still open, and everything was as they left it, following the shooting. Skee found his hat under the rocking-chair. They looked the place over, closed the door and rode back to Encinitas.

Flint Harper and his men came in early, as did Duncan Wheeler, bringing Bill Long and Frenchy Allard with him. Orville Woodruff slept late, but got up feeling fairly well. He was stiff and sore, but thankful to be alive.

He could add nothing to his original story. It was his impression that Topete was working alone, because his was the only voice he heard. Orville was positive that he rode at least two hours, coming from his place of captivity to Encinitas. He was anxious to see Micky and Spook, who did not come to Encinitas until after the noon hour.

Micky seemed tired and grim, as he listened to Orville's story, while the cowboys crowded in close to listen again. Micky looked at Flint Harper as he remarked:

'I reckon you know now how it feels to have somebody tryin' to break you, Harper.'

Flint Harper did not reply; so Duncan Wheeler said:

'Don'tcha think it's kinda funny—Topete askin' that you bring him the money?'

'Not very funny, Dunc. In that way he can kill two birds with one stone: get the money and kill me, too.'

'Would you refuse to take the money?' asked the sheriff.

'How could I refuse? If my life would bring Norma home—I'd pay the price. But it won't. The money would be gone, and Norma wouldn't come home.'

'What do you think of Topete turnin' Woodruff loose to act as a messenger?' asked Wheeler.

'I think he was smart,' replied Micky. 'If Topete can't write—it was his only way of makin' a demand.'

'He told me he couldn't write,' said Orville.

Spook Sullivan leaned against the bar. He fussed with his cartridge belt and adjusted his holster carefully. There was a queer expression on Spook's face, a sort of grim smile. His lips were tightly compressed. Micky looked at him, then looked away, a faint smile on his tight lips.

'I was over at the bank a few minutes ago, Flint,' said Wheeler. 'It might be possible for them to furnish part of the money—mebbe all of it—in a case like this. It would take all the Circle H to handle the deal. I dunno—they might. It wouldn't hurt to find out.'

'If you only had a chance to talk with Topete—you—'

'Why *not* talk to Topete?' asked Micky tensely. 'He's here!'

For a moment no one moved. They had been too interested to hear a man come through the rear doorway of the saloon.

'Here?' whispered Flint Harper.

'Turn around!' snapped Micky.

About halfway between the crowd and the back doorway stood Topete in his bedraggled finery, a tired-looking figure, but smiling.

'*Buenas dias, amigos,*' he said huskily.

'Don't shoot,' warned Micky. 'He's as innocent as you are.'

'Damnation!' muttered Duncan Wheeler. He jerked away from the crowd, drawing his gun, while Frenchy and Bill Long whirled toward the doorway, clawing at their guns, cursing bitterly.

Micky's first shot drove Duncan Wheeler into a card table and he went to his knees. Spook was shooting swiftly. Frenchy Allard went down, crashing into a chair. Bill Long's bullets raised havoc with the glassware on the back bar, until he flung up both hands and fell out into the street when Micky's flaming gun spouted lead at his huge body.

Spook leaned back against the bar, wiping blood from one cheek where it had been cut by flying glass. A bullet had creased Micky's left forearm, and blood was dripping off his fingers.

Then the crowd, white-faced, shocked to inaction, took a deep breath. The bartender, dripping perspiration and broken glass, raised up from behind the bar. There was someone yelling outside the saloon. Skee Harris cried sharply as he looked through the doorway:

'Norma! Flint, there's Norma out there—in the street!'

Flint Harper went out like a drunken man, stepped over Bill Long's feet, and met Norma in the street.

'Great heavens! What does it mean?' blurted the sheriff. 'Micky, what is it?'

'You better put handcuffs on Wheeler,' said Micky. 'He's worse than a blind rattler.'

'I'll get him, Micky!' gasped Skee.

Duncan Wheeler spat a curse at Skee, who quickly handcuffed him. Frenchy Allard was dead, and Bill Long was dying. Topete moved in beside Micky.

'*Amigo*,' he said quietly, theese ees w'at you call the beeg clean-up, huh?'

Doctor Mitchell came quickly. He was so shocked that he could hardly make an examination. He had known and respected Duncan

Wheeler for years. The prosecuting attorney arrived. Duncan refused to tell anything, even when the doctor told him he did not have over an hour to live.

Miguel Topete remained silent, refusing to answer questions. He merely pointed at Micky and said:

'My *amigo* talk for me.'

Flint Harper came back into the saloon. He shook hands with Micky, but seemed unable to say anything. The prosecutor came to Micky.

'Davis,' he said, 'I guess you are the only one who can tell the story. All Norma knows is that you found her at Duncan Wheeler's ranch, hidden away in an old garret, along with Topete and the old Mexican woman this morning.'

'That's the story,' replied Micky quietly.

'But how on earth did you figure that out—when no one else even had such a suspicion? You must have had something to base such a belief on, Davis?'

Quietly, Micky explained about his and Spook's finding the hidden trail into Lobo Solo and what happened to them down there.

'I thought that Flint Harper was workin' with Topete,' said Micky. 'Then when Topete robbed Ed Ross that night, I smelled a mouse. Why would Topete wear a mask? It didn't work out. When I had to kill Manuel Ramirez, I felt sure that he wasn't workin' for Harper, but I didn't quite understand, 'cause I knew damn well that Manuel was the Mexican who had the fight with Orville Woodruff.

'When Topete was rescued from the jail, killed my horse, and fired the stable, after takin' his palomino, I didn't believe Topete did it. I didn't have no proof, but it looked like somebody was puttin' the deadwood too heavy on Topete.

'Buck, me and Spook saw that shootin' at the ranch last night. Yeah; we was hidin' out down there, and we didn't know who either party was until we found Skee's hat. After you was gone, I found the rifle shells, where they pumped 'em out on the ground, and one gun shore put a queer mark on the primer.

'Me and Spook came here last night, and I stole the rifle out of Frenchy Allard's scabbard. Then me and Spook went plumb around to the other side of Lobo Solo, went down that deer trail and over to the other trail, where we found the shells that were fired at us. They were the same as some of the shells fired at you and Skee; and the rifle we stole from Frenchy was the gun that fired 'em.'

'Clever deductions,' applauded the prosecutor.

'Yeah!' snorted Spook. 'You just try goin' down that deer trail in the dark.'

'Well, it wasn't so hard—after that,' said Micky. 'We came out of the canyon, rode over to the Box JB, and waited until Wheeler, Allard, and

Long rode away. If you stop to think about it, Bill Long and Miguel Topete are built a lot alike.'

'How on earth did they expect to get away with the ransom idea?' asked the sheriff.

'Take the money, kill me off—and Norma would never come back. You see, in that struggle at my ranch between Norma and Bill Long, Norma tore his mask off. You can see now why she'd never have been allowed to come back.'

'Wheeler wants to talk,' said the doctor.

They walked to the back of the room, where the doctor had placed Wheeler on a cot.

'I reckon this is the finish,' he said weakly. 'Doc says I'm livin' on borrowed time right now, so I'm willin' to talk.'

'You killed Jack Woodruff, Wheeler,' said Micky.

'I reckon I did,' replied Wheeler. 'No use implicatin' anybody else. I—I wanted that mine. We thought the kid might have information—through that old letter—so we took him off the stage. I don't reckon the mine will ever be found.'

'Where did Jack Woodruff live around here?' asked Micky.

'Out there on your place, Davis. That old shack next to your stable was his house.'

'What did you fellows think when you saw me and Spook, after you blasted the canyon trail, Wheeler?'

'We—we figured that the dynamite didn't knock it down.'

'I reckon that's all I want to know,' said Micky.

The prosecutor leaned over Wheeler and said:

'Have you any relatives, Wheeler; anybody to give your property?'

'No. I—I—don't know who—Where's Micky Davis? Give it to him. I tried to break him. He's got—brains. Whipped me with the mark on an empty shell. Give it—to—Micky.'

For several moments there was silence. Then the sheriff said:

'Would a will like that hold in law?'

'With a dozen witnesses—yes,' replied the lawyer.

Micky took Orville by the arm and they walked outside, followed by Spook and Topete. Norma was with her father and the Circle H cowboys, together with many more interested people, including Grandma Ramirez.

Micky went to the old lady and put an arm around her shoulder.

'You're not goin' back to Mexico,' he told her. 'You'll be part of my gang as long as you live.'

Micky turned to the crowd and said:

'Manuel Ramirez worked for Wheeler and his gang. He knew too much, so they tried to kill him; but he got away, managed to get home, and sent the old lady to tell me who stole my calves. Then he came back to clean up on them—and made a mistake.'

Norma stepped over to Micky. 'Grandma Ramirez told me about you bringing her presents, Micky,' she said. 'I'm sorry—I believed what was told me.'

'Shucks, that's all right,' smiled Micky. 'We all made mistakes. Flint, I admit that I was mistaken about you. I hope there will be peace between my outfit and yours.'

Flint Harper looked at Micky and then at Norma.

'Well, I don't know why there shouldn't be,' he said soberly. 'I'm not the kind to fight my own relatives—even by marriage.'

Orville Woodruff walked in and shook hands solemnly with Micky.

'I—I guess I'll be going back to San Francisco,' he said. 'I've certainly had a fine time down here, and I—'

'Goin' where?' snorted Micky. 'Why, you double barrel idiot, you've got the richest gold mine on earth.'

'I know; but it's under your shed, Micky.'

'For the love o' mud!' exploded Micky. 'Red, I'll move the shed for you.'

'You mean—Well! Micky, I'd—How about you and Spook and me owning that mine? We'll share alike. And we'll call it the Topete mine. He really should get at least that much out of it, Micky.'

Topete smiled slowly and shook his head.

'For my own personal self I want notheeng,'

he said. 'I mak' beeg meestake one time when I try kees beauteeful *señorita*. But *por Dios*, could I be blame' for that? I wan' to thank those men who don' theenk I am worth more than five thousand pesos, biccause theese Beel Long he tells me that w'en theese reward ees beeg enough, they weel keel me and mak' collection. Now I'm theenk I go back to *Mejico* and be damn honest cowman. I can leeve longer, I theenk.'

'Go ahead, Miguel,' said the sheriff laughing. 'You're all right.'

'Everything is all right,' added Flint Harper.

'Ain't that true!' exclaimed Spook. 'Why, Micky, you can—Listen! With a third interest in that gold mine, the Bar D, and the Box JB, you can walk into that danged bank and tell 'em—'

'Why tell 'em anythin'?' interrupted Micky. 'We'll buy the darned thing.'

'Micky,' reminded Flint Harper, 'I offered ten thousand dollars reward for Norma, alive and well. You've earned it—and more.'

'I'll take *more,*' grinned Micky, 'and you can keep your money.'

Micky put his arm around Norma, and they walked over toward the buckboard, which they had brought from the Box JB. Flint Harper shook his head and smiled widely. It was not often that Flint Harper smiled.

'If you remember rightly, Buck,' he said to the

sheriff, 'I said we needed brains more than brawn to solve this mystery.'

'I knowed it all along,' interposed Spook, 'but it took me quite a while to get settled down to thinkin' real hard.'

'Thinkin' about what?' asked the sheriff quickly.

Spook cuffed his hat over one eye and thoughtfully scratched his left cheek for several moments. Then he turned to Orville.

'If you're ready to go back to the ranch, let's pull out. We'll have to start early in the mornin' takin' them calves out of Lobo Solo, before they starve to death. Micky's done forgot 'em. Hell, he's even forgot there is a Lobo Solo Canyon. Brains! Right now he ain't got the brains of a chickadee.'

Spook glared at the two people in the buckboard, which was turning away from the hitch rack.

'He is rather a likable idiot, though,' said Orville quietly.

Spook chuckled quickly, cuffed his hat over his eyes, and scratched the back of his lean neck.

'I hope to tell you,' he said soberly.

Center Point Large Print
600 Brooks Road / PO Box 1
Thorndike, ME 04986-0001 USA

(207) 568-3717

US & Canada:
1 800 929-9108
www.centerpointlargeprint.com